THE OLD PHOTOGRAPHS TOLD TINA THE STORY . . .

A much younger Scott Welles looked out from the photograph with soft, loving eyes. In the next picture was the girl who possessed that love—Sinjuko, smiling gravely into the camera. Then Sinjuko cooking over a square hole in the floor. Sinjuko in front of a shrine at a place called Nikho. Sinjuko pouring tea. Sinjuko of the lovely face, the dark almond eyes. The white teeth. The silken hair . . .

That had been twenty years ago. *But what wife*, Tina Welles asked herself, *could compete with such a memory?*

A few days later Tina was dead . . . murdered . . . and now it was the police who asked the same question.

THE JAPANESE MISTRESS

"INTRIGUING . . . GOES BEYOND THE TYPICAL WHODUNIT IN ITS PROBING OF THE INTIMATE AND SOMETIMES PERVERSE RELATIONS BETWEEN PEOPLE."
—Grand Rapids Press

Also by RICHARD NEELY
from Jove/HBJ BOOKS

**LIES
NO CERTAIN LIFE**

THE JAPANESE MISTRESS

RICHARD NEELY

A JOVE HBJ BOOK

To Jill, Scott, Steven and Dick
with love

Copyright © 1972 by Richard Neely

All rights reserved. No part of this publication may be reproduced or transmitted in any form or by any means, electronic or mechanical, including photocopy, recording, or any information storage and retrieval system, without permission in writing from the publisher.

Printed in the United States of America

Library of Congress Catalog Card Number: 78-182482

First Jove/HBJ edition published June 1979

Jove/HBJ books are published by Jove Publications, Inc. (Harcourt Brace Jovanovich), 757 Third Avenue, New York, NY 10017

Tokyo

1947

I

T/3 SCOTT WELLES 39443718

Armed Forces Information Service
Information & Education Detachment
General Headquarters
Armed Forces Pacific

Notes for a Novel

The young American soldier and the Japanese girl (she was eighteen) stood on the crowded El platform waiting for the train that would take them to her home for his first meeting with her parents. Behind them, on another track, a decrepit all-Japanese train had been stopped and the passengers herded to the platform where American medics with wide hoses were shooting DDT down the necks of their clothing, as if delousing animals. The passengers accepted the treatment with impassive docility. The Japanese girl kept her eyes lowered, pretending unawareness, but the soldier sensed her pain; the foot of space separating them seemed to stretch to a yard.

Their train clattered in and he had to put pressure on her upper arm to guide her into one of the cars technically restricted to Allied personnel. Half a dozen other soldiers were aboard, two with Japanese girls dressed in skirts and sweaters. At the sight of them, his girl settled more comfortably on the seat and smiled shyly at him.

They had known each other for six weeks, and

though they felt excitement in each other's presence, though they often exchanged admiring looks, they had never intimately touched. Once when he had seen a heavily powdered, high-coiffed Japanese girl laughing on the Ginza with a group of Australian soldiers, he had asked, "Geisha?" "No," she had answered. "*Makura*—pillow geisha." The way she had said it—a mixture of sadness and pity—told him that it was a role she would not allow herself to play. *Koibito*—sweetheart—perhaps, but never a pillow geisha.

They got off at Akabane station and walked down broad stone steps to where a cluster of open-fronted wooden stalls housed vendors displaying dried fish and stunted vegetables. Then down a winding dirt road, their feet kicking up puffs of dust, to a colony of wood-and-paper cottages, all alike and set close together in two parallel lines. Ditches filled with brackish water ran in front of the houses and a scattering of women squatted beside them washing clothes and children. Seeing the American approach, they quickly abandoned their chores and scurried into their homes, smiling and somehow managing to bow. The girl looked up at him and said, "*Hazakashii*" —embarrassed.

They stepped across the ditch and she took his hand as if to give him confidence and led him to the side of her house. Without her knocking or speaking, a tan shoji screen slid open and he gazed expectantly into a bare interior. Looking down, he saw two people on the floor, a man and a woman. They were on their knees, bodies and arms stretched out, foreheads touching the shiny straw mat.

He put down the rucksack he was carrying and timidly said good evening: "*Komban wa!*"

The two prostrated figures raised their faces, beamed in pleasure, and said several times. "*Yoku irasshaimashita!*" Welcome! Welcome! Welcome!

They then withdrew as the girl gently tugged him down on the single step and took off his shoes. They entered a small, square room lit by a solitary green-shaded bulb that hung from a wire in the ceiling, illuminating a gridded square hole in the floor, on which stood a steaming kettle. Mama-san and Papa-san sat beside it on worn red pillows, facing each other. They motioned him to sit between them. He did, feeling stiff and awkward. The girl elaborated on the introductions, speaking softly in Japanese to her parents, who looked seriously at her and then at him in bright approval. Like almost all Japanese, they were quite small, the father no more than five feet, the mother a couple of inches shorter. He was a squarely built man, but with no excess flesh, his arms below the short sleeves of his black kimono lean and sinewy. His graying hair was cropped close, and he wore metal-rimmed glasses which gave his thin-mouthed face a sinister look, but his manner was affable and outgoing. The mother, also in a black kimono, might have been called petite, except that she too had corded arms, and her face, still faintly pretty, was lined in a way that suggested great endurance, often tested.

She poured green tea into small, white, handleless cups set on a low red-laquered table next to her. They waited until their guest had sipped and said his memorized *"Oishii"*—delicious—before smilingly accompanying him. He then whipped out his phrase book and soon they were all jabbering away in mostly unrelated phrases, often misunderstanding, constantly laughing, but still warmly communicating. Once, Papa-san said something in Japanese and ended with the word "Boolshit." Startled and delighted, the American asked the girl to translate. "Papa-san want to know why American soldiers all the time say 'boolshit.'" She grinned mischievously. "You translate?" He looked up the word "lie" and said, *"Uso."*

They ate a skimped-down version of tempura, and brown rice, and beef in gravy from the canned C-rations he had brought. Then, as Mama-san almost invisibly cleaned up, he signaled to the girl and she brought from his rucksack a fifth of Old Suntory whiskey. At first the two men drank alone and smoked Chesterfields provided by the American. Papa-san made sucking and sighing noises to indicate his pleasure at this extravagant show of generosity. He had been a minor executive in a silk mill, converted some years before to the manufacture of parachutes, but now, in defeat, he was out of a job. When the two women joined them with small portions of whiskey—Mama-san hungrily puffing a cigarette—the girl explained that they had previously lived in another, much larger house. "Then come B-29's," she said. "And *whooosh!* no more house. *Kajida!*—fire." Her parents understood and laughed so that the American would not be offended. He felt a wave of shame.

The girl's brother arrived, dressed in a black high-collared uniform. He worked for the railroad, clearing the roadbeds, and had just finished for the day. He was a grinning, good-natured boy of fourteen, very polite, openly admiring the American—once touching the crisp sleeve of his uniform—and addressing him self-consciously with spurts of faltering English. A little later, the sister came, a tiny baby nursing at her breast, and was overwhelmed with shyness at meeting the American. She was twenty-two, married to a salesman who was on a long business trip in the southern island of Kyushu, and she lived five doors away. It turned out that only a few hours before she had been threatened with tragedy: her milk had suddenly dried up, which could have meant the death of her baby. Twenty minutes ago, it had started to flow again. After telling her story, she left, murmuring effusive apologies.

It was past ten o'clock when he rose to leave. The girl spoke quietly and rapidly to her parents in Japanese. They glanced at each other with looks of understanding, then together nodded in assent. "You stay all night," the girl said. "We have other room. Not big but okay."

The room, separated from the main one by a sliding screen, was long and narrow and opened to the rear of the house. The girl made a bed of silk quilts stretched on a sleeping mat. Handing him a lightweight purple kimono, she stood looking up at him in the soft light filtering in from the other room. Her hand reached out slowly and touched his cheek. He started to bend to her but she dropped her hand and took a step backward. "I must go speak to family," she said. Smiling, she left him.

He undressed and donned the kimono, which was short and loosely comfortable. He slipped beneath the silken quilt, hearing whispered voices on the other side of the screen. Apparently they were holding a family council. Soon the light inside went out, leaving him in pale moonlight. He rolled over on his side, facing away from the screen, and pillowed his head on his arm. He closed his eyes, but resisted sleep to think about the girl, her shining liquid eyes, her gentleness, the delicacy of form that he could only imagine. His ear caught a sliding sound. He stirred. A sudden tangible warmth nestled against his back. Then a breath in his ear, floating the words, "Family say it is okay."

He turned, dimly seeing her kimono heaped on the floor as his arm went around her. "Oh yes, yes," he said, "it is *takusan*—much—okay."

There were no awkward fumblings, no hesitant movements. It was as though they had apprenticed for this long past the point of mere competency and were eager to demonstrate their skills lavishly for the other's approval. When finally he entered her, when they reached the excruciating brute pitch that could no longer be borne, when they gave all that could physically be given and clung together like a single exhausted body, he felt that he had known the glory of her, if only in fantasy, since the beginning of his manhood.

Later she said, "My first time," but not in a tone that sought to convince.

He believed her, but was curious. "You were so ... so knowing."

"Pictures," she said ingenuously. "Japanese art. And talks with Sister and Mama-san."

They found each other again during the black night, and again in the gray dawn, and she showed him how thoroughly she had studied Japanese art and how wise were her sister and Mama-san.

The next time they met she gravely handed him a small slip of paper.

"From doctor," she said, and turned her face away.

It took him a few moments to understand that it indicated the results of a test she had taken for venereal disease. A check mark was inked in the square that read NEGATIVE.

"So you feel safe," she said shyly.

Three or four evenings a week he would take the El to Akabane station where she would be waiting on the platform. He carried two bulging rucksacks now, one loaded with C-rations and cans of fruit donated by the mess sergeant of the Mitsubishi building, where he was officially quartered, the other packed with winter G.I. clothing, no longer issued in June— long johns, O.D. pants and sweaters, knitted caps— provided by a nisei friend. The women squatting beside the ditches no longer scurried away at his approach; instead they smiled and waved salutes, and called out softly, "*Komban wa!*" He had become an accepted member of the community. The girl held tightly to his arm, her face radiant.

Inside the house, the rucksack with the food would be put away, but he would zip open the other and ceremoniously display the garments on the tatami floor, like some Arab in a bazarr. Then he would drape the longjohns against his body as if modeling them, or maybe pull a knitted cap low on his forehead, frowning fiercely, and his hosts would laugh hilariously but with gratitude. To Brother he would say, "You dye everything black—*kuroi*—so M.P. not know." The clothing would not be used until the cold came in the fall, and the thought gave him a pang. He might then be gone.

At night he and the girl alternated between sleeping and making love in the narrow room. Without words, as if reading each other's minds, they came together in every conceivable way, until they found the ones that suited them best. She seemed to anticipate his every need and desire; sometimes, without him asking, massaging his back, sometimes stroking his loins, sometimes dropping the top of her kimono and offering him her breast—"your toy."

If it was Saturday or Sunday, she would give him a morning bath—a makeshift affair because they had no deep-sunken tile tub. She would heat pails of water on the firepit in the floor and bring them to where he stood naked outside an open screen, on a wooden ledge that ran the length of the house. Clad only in white cotton panties, she would douse him with water, then join him on the ledge and lather him with PX soap. Then she would rinse him off and towel him until he was dry and tingling.

Later, he would work in the vegetable garden with the girl and her mother. It was a pathetic patch, cleared from rubble and carved into scorched earth. The produce it yielded appeared aborted. In the afternoons, they would laze about the house, drinking tea, perhaps playing checkers, sometimes making love, and later take a walk.

He felt very important and very much loved. He realized that he could not have felt that way had he not given importance and love to another.

Sausalito

1968

II

Catherine breathed a long sigh and placed the yellow manuscript carefully on the bed beside her. There was more to be read, but now she felt a need to adjust to the weird sensation that she had just met her father for the first time. There was no doubt in her mind that the American in the story *was* her father—not only because he was the author, but also because of the way he acted with the Japanese people—the way he was with her.

She hiked up on the pillow, curving her arms around her zoo—a huge stuffed tiger with a foolish grin and an equally huge lion with a shaggy mane almost as blonde as her own, though not nearly so long. Glancing at the electric clock on the night table, she saw it was almost five: she had at least an hour before Tina—*Mother*, she corrected herself—would arrive home from the tennis club. More time than was needed to shuck her faded blue jeans and orange T-shirt, comb her hair, don the pastel dress she had worn until her mother had left at noon, and appear at the door with a smiling greeting.

Every weekday she went through the same deceit, her guilt eased somewhat by the unspoken approval of Helen, the housekeeper, who came in at ten and left shortly after six. Weekends the jeans and T-shirt were tolerated because her father would be home and the two of them would be off hiking, fishing, or driving to explore the beaches and wooded hills surrounding San Francisco Bay. Her mother would usually spend most of Saturday and Sunday at the tennis club, a place, Catherine knew, her father hated and that she had seen only when driving by.

The thought of her mother triggered a shiver of apprehension as she recalled where the story and the pictures had been found—in an old, gouged, green footlocker at the very back of the storage closet opposite her parents' bedroom. Once before she had entered that closet, shining a flashlight over the odds and ends of cast-off furniture, pretending they were trees and that she was lost in a dark wood, waiting for a rescuer. The fantasy had ended explosively when her frantic mother had burst in, yanked her out, and scolded her terribly for "deliberately trying to drive me mad!"

Awful, awful boredom had led her, a little earlier, to enter the closet again. She had been at the head of the stairs, about to go down to the kitchen, hoping to have a cup of tea with Helen, when she noticed the door standing ajar. Before she realized it, she was bumping against ghostly shapes, soon bending over what looked like an oblong wooden box and pulling at an ancient lock that released a light shower of rust as it grated open. And there they were: khaki pants, shirt, cap, a green jacket, like a windbreaker—the clothes worn by her father during the Japanese Occupation. And wrapped in them, a sheaf of papers entitled "Notes for a Novel," and pictures of a lot of Japanese people in bathrobes—no, kimonos. She had replaced the garments in the footlocker, adjusting the padlock so that it appeared secure, and rushed back to her bedroom with her treasures.

It had been impossible to imagine her father dressed in those strange clothes. She could see him only in his beautifully tailored business suit, tie knotted perfectly in the V of his white shirt; or handsomely casual in slacks and sweater on weekends. But now there was no need for imagination. Clad in uniform, he was smiling up at her from the top of the stack of pictures, eyes soft and affectionate. She was astonished that he had changed so little; perhaps now the face was a little less smooth and the figure a little less thin. How old had he been then? This being 1968 and her father forty-three, he would have been about twenty-two back then.

She picked up the handful of pictures, which she had only riffled through before, set aside the one of her father, and looked at the next. Four Japanese, two men, two women, their faces expressionless. She was about to place it on the bed when she noticed some writing on the back; "Papa-san, Mama-san, Sinjuko, Brudda." Brudda? Maybe her father had meant "Brother" but wrote it the way they said it. He had sometimes imitated the way many Japanese spoke English. She laughed and stretched out prone on the bed, resting on her elbows. Slowly, completely fascinated, she started through the rest of the pictures, reading the short inscriptions on the backs.

The girl in the first Japanese picture appeared in most of the others, generally alone. Catherine turned back to the foursome and read her name again, pressing her tongue against her teeth to pronounce it—Sinjuko. She looked like an older teen-ager, very pretty, with straight black hair reaching not quite to her shoulders. . . .

Sinjuko cooking over a square hole in the floor. Sinjuko in front of a shrine at a place called Nikko. Sinjuko gazing up at a huge Buddha in Kamakura. Sinjuko pouring tea. Sinjuko sitting in a contraption called a ginricksha.

Finally Catherine came to another picture of her father alone. She gasped. He was standing on a narrow ledge that ran along the side of a Japanese house.

His back was to the camera and he was grinning over his shoulder. He was stark naked. The note said, "This is where I get my bath. The water is poured from a big oak bucket."

Just as it was in the story! She felt a warm flush creep up her slim body, cresting to her cheeks. The one who had swung the oak bucket—the girl in the cotton panties—must have been Sinjuko! Why else would the girl be in so many of the pictures? And the others—Mama-san, Papa-san, Brudda—they also were the ones in the story. She should have understood that right away.

She sorted through the snapshots and withdrew all those of Sinjuko, arranging them in a row on the bed. Gravely she examined the lovely face. The dark almond eyes. The white teeth when she smiled. The silken hair. The erect posture. She looked like a Japanese doll that Catherine had once admired in a store, the one she would have bought if her mother hadn't talked her into a Barbie Doll instead.

Her thoughts were interrupted by the sound of an approaching car. She jumped up and hop-skipped to the long window facing the back of the house and gazed down through the boughs of the live oaks, dappled now by the descending June sun, to where the sloping bank ended in the black road. No kids were playing there. Most of them, she guessed, were spending the summer vacation at Lake Tahoe or Russian River. She pushed her small nose to the pane and saw a jalopy whiz past. Disappointed, she turned away, realizing that it was too early for her father. But there had been a time, long ago, when he had often arrived home before her mother and had played games with her and told her wonderful stories. There were still the play and the stories, but now they always came later, just before her bedtime.

She brightened as she returned to the bed, this time picking up the manuscript. Now she had a clear picture of the girl in the story—Sinjuko.

Stretching out, she again began to read.

Tokyo

1947

III

The July heat was withering, and at night the mosquitoes arrived in hordes. Now he and the girl had to sleep in the main room with the rest of the family because they lacked enough mosquito netting for the private room. The green netting was hung from the ceiling and arranged into three tentlike sections, one for the parents, one for brother, and one for him and the girl.

A week of that and there was another family council. He strolled out to the vegetable garden while they put their heads together beneath the cone of light. Soon he saw Mama-san and Papa-san leave through the side door and hurry down the street. He went back inside. "Papa-san, Mama-san be back soon," was all the girl said. She got up, poured him a cup of sake, and reached for the checkerboard.

They had finished two games and were starting another when her parents returned, both trying to suppress smiles. They bowed to him apologetically before speaking to their daughter in Japanese. When they finished, they all turned to him with beaming faces, the girl hugging herself in delight.

"Everything is okay," she said. "We move."

"Move?"

"*Hai!* You, me, we move to Sister's house. Sister and baby come live here, until husband come back."

An hour later, after Brother had arrived, they moved, all four escorting him down the dark road, each carrying an article of clothing, a kitchen utensil, or some knick-knack. Sister greeted them at the sliding door, her eyes shimmering as she bowed low in welcome. Removing his shoes, he entered as if walking through some wondrous dream. The house was almost a duplicate of the one they had left, with one startling exception. Sister led him to it with fluttering waves of her hand. It was a battered Western-style wooden desk complete with scarred leather swivel chair.

The girl looked at him glowingly. "Neighbor give it," she said. "Now you have place to work at home."

Home. He felt his eyes moisten and was unable to speak. They all understood how deeply touched he was and were happy.

They were joyous in what he called, searching his word book, *Shinkon-ryoko Ie*—Honeymoon House. Each morning when he wakened, he felt that he owned the day. There were no pressures. As a writer for *Maptalk*, the Supreme Command Allied Powers publication that provided troop information relevant to the Occupation, he found his work constantly satisfying, often quietly exciting, a product of himself and sponsored by a great historic happening. Much of what he did could be accomplished at home, the girl never interrupting or making a sound, but always *there*, her love permeating the small house.

It was mid-August when she became sick. She had been wan and listless for more than a week but had attributed it to nothing more than the heat. Then the coughing started and the cold sweating. A Japanese doctor was summoned—a thin old man with horn-rimmed glasses and a small white goatee. The family squatted around her feet as her temperature was taken, her chest listened to and thumped, her eyelids stretched and examined. The doctor then paced about in a circle, stroked his goatee, hissed a few times, and gave his diagnosis.

She had a temperature of 102 degrees, not serious but it must not be allowed to continue. She had probably picked up some sort of germ—new types seemed to be appearing every day, spawned by the devastation—but he was sure it could be subdued. He wrote out instructions and left some pills and small packets of medicines to be brewed in tea. Then, bowing and striving to exude confidence but failing, he left.

Mama-san came to nurse her, sleeping on the floor in the adjoining room. The next day the temperature had risen a point. Following instructions, they gave her a tepid bath, rolling her onto a green oilskin and swabbing her with soaked towels. Mama-san confined herself to the limbs, politely leaving the private parts to him. The girl lifted her arm weakly and patted him on the head, saying with teasing affection, "*Utsukushii kangofu-san*"—beautiful nurse. When he reached the pubic area, her lips hooked into a small grin and she said, "Ah so . . . new way!" He smiled back but was frightened.

The next day the doctor returned and found that her temperature was no lower. Pulling at his goatee, he meditated. Finally he said, "*Byoin*"—and a look of despair crossed his face.

The American thumbed through his language book. *Byoin* meant hospital. He stared at the doctor, saw the helpless shrug and the extended index finger moving horizontally in the air, signifying no. It was apparent that in whatever remained of Japanese hospitals no beds were available. The doctor handed out more medicine and left, his face sad, his shoulders sagging.

The girl said to him, "Doctor say not to worry. I will be okay."

He looked at her mother. Her black eyes were like hard chunks of coal. Panic spurted through him.

He spoke to his commanding officer the next morning. He told the captain everything, knowing him to be an intelligent, compassionate, to-hell-with-it sort of man who didn't give a damn about regulations.

The captain's immediate response was, "Jesus Christ, I'm supposed to be going home next week! For *discharge!* Jesus Christ, I don't want to screw that up!"

"I thought you might know a doctor who would be willing to help."

"Two of 'em are my buddies. But asking them to smuggle her into an American army hospital! Jesus Christ!"

"She's not just any Japanese girl."

"I know that. But Jesus Christ, an American army hospital! Old Dugout Doug would personally have my ass!"

He waited as the captain yanked off his steel-rimmed glasses, blew on them, polished them on his sleeve, flung them back on, rubbed at his blond crewcut.

"All right," he said finally. "I'll give it a try. That's a promise. But Jee-sus *Christ!*"

The next morning the captain handed him a requisition permitting him to check out a weapons carrier from the motor pool. "That's your ambulance." He wrote down some directions. "Here's how to get to the hospital. Jesus Christ! Captain Wilson Robinette, a Park Avenue doctor, will meet you there after dark tonight—about nine P.M. He hates this shitty army and is delirious with joy at being able to shaft it if only just a little bit, especially in the name of humanitarianism. An American army hospital! Jee-sus *Ka-rist!*"

At eight o'clock that night he and Papa-san lifted her feverish body gingerly into the back of the weapons carrier and laid her on a stack of silk quilts.

Just the two of them made the trip, he driving slowly, trying to steer around chuck holes in the pitch blackness, and peering over his shoulder at intervals to murmur reassurances.

They were met outside the hospital by Dr. Robinette, a tall, cadaverous man with devilish eyes and a thin mouth set in a look of grim satisfaction.

Somehow he had managed to have her admitted to a small private room.

A week later, on a Saturday evening, he brought her home. Her cheeks had rounded out and her eyes were clear and sparkling and she had only a remnant of the cough. He had visited her every day after work, sneaking in the side entrance to avoid the reception desk. Once, after her temperature had become normal, she had persuaded him to lock the door and join her in the high hospital bed. He had been very gentle with her—gentler than she wanted, he knew—and though it was nothing like what they had experienced at home, it was still wonderful.

When they got home, and after the family had lovingly welcomed her and left, they enjoyed each other in all the old ways, which seemed awesomely new. Then he handed her an envelope. Opening it, she stared at the two train tickets to Nikko and her black eyes rounded in wonder. Tears spilled down her cheeks and she flung herself against him and he caressed her sublime nakedness.

His three-day pass started on Wednesday and they caught the eight A.M. train at Ueno station. They carried three bulging rucksacks, his two containing the food and whiskey, hers the changes of clothing. (She had made a mock-sad clucking noise. "Clothes? Why wear clothes? *Takusan waruii!*"—very bad.)

Early as it was, the station was thronged. They stood in a long line outside the gate where a self-important Japanese checked the people through. Many of the travelers wore white gauze masks across their noses and mouths to ward off germs. Some women had babies strapped to their backs; others carried huge straw baskets in the knapsack position (to haul vegetables and fruit from the country, the girl said). A seamed old lady was stopped officiously by the guard, who examined her ticket and turned her away. The American strode forward, waved a finger at the guard and spoke to him harshly. The guard looked startled. The old woman went through. Back in line, the girl asked him what he said. "I said, 'I tell MacArthur!'" The girl clapped her hands together in delight.

The train they boarded, though shabby, resembled the coaches in the States. He went ahead into the car reserved for military personnel and spoke to the M.P. "No sweat, buddy," the M.P. said. "Bring her aboard. To me, she's from Kansas City." So they sat in the G.I. car that was only about a third filled, in the very last seat where she would feel inconspicuous.

The train bucked and jerked as they pulled out of the station, then settled to an even clickety-clack as it reached open country, a leveled wasteland that seemed to reach to infinity, with only the bent backs of people scrounging through the blackened rubble to certify that this was a part of Earth. In an hour, the devastation was behind them and they began to climb. Soon they were flanked by a forest, so green it hurt the eyes, and close enough to reach out and touch. The track circled and rose, and looking through the window glass, cheeks pressed together, they could see the distant engine puffing clouds of smoke as it labored up a steep grade. The forest thinned and they came upon farmhouses made of bamboo caulked with clay, with straw-thatched roofs, and occasionally there was a scrawny cow or a few flapping ducks in the yards. They climbed higher and entered the semimarine world of the rice paddies, where men and women wearing conical hats woven of yellow straw straightened from their labors grinning and waving. At every new sight the girl made small sounds of pleasure, squeezing his hand and telling him with glowing eyes of her enjoyment. Gazing at the sheer mountains, he remarked that the Japanese must have to hold on with one hand and farm with the other. She thought that enormously funny and repeated it several times, stifling her laughter with the tips of her fingers, as they sped through the green and gold morning.

They reached Nikko in mid-afternoon. At the small station building, its red paint baked to a veined pink, they were met by a fat man in brown shirt and pants and a cap with a shiny broken peak—the taxi driver. He snatched up the three rucksacks, shouted *"Hubba-hubba,"* and led them to a battered green car with big fenders and running boards, smoke pouring from the rear. They sat on rusted springs that had burst through the threadbare fabric and went bucketing off in a whirl of dust and smoke.

The infernal machine bounced them down a long straight road and in a few minutes exploded to a stop in front of a two-story structure of wood and rice paper that was the inn. Two broad matted stairs led to a lobby devoid of furniture and open to the outdoors. A thin, balding man with a yellow beard, the manager, came forward, bowed low to them both and bid them good afternoon. They sat on the step in the sun while children in bright kimonos took their shoes and whisked them away. Women fitted them with straw slippers and a teen-age girl led them inside and up narrow highly polished stairs and down a short hall. She slid open a screen, stood aside, bowed, and gestured them inside. They removed their slippers and entered a square room furnished, only with the usual red-lacquered table and several outsized silk pillows. Their three rucksacks had been placed in a corner. The maid followed them in and slid open another screen, revealing a small balcony overlooking the main street. She scurried away and was back in a few minutes bearing a copper brazier heaped with soft charcoal which she set on the table. She opened a tiny closet, drew out two lightweight blue and white kimonos, presented them, bowed, and was gone.

He sat on a big green pillow, back against the wall, sipping a drink and watching as she undressed. Naked, she stood erectly in front of him, bowed ceremoniously, and announced with elaborate solemnity, "I now give you very fine entertainment." With that she danced about the room, twirling and kicking her legs as she had once seen the precision dancers do at the Ernie Pyle Theater. Choking with laughter, he got up and she whirled into his arms, bursting into joyous giggles. He undressed and they donned the short kimonos and went out on the balcony. They smoked cigarettes and gazed up at the green peaks spired with firs, speaking little but saying much with their eyes and their touch. Then they went back inside and delighted each other with very fine entertainment.

The maid came with a large tray bearing plates heaped with gravied chunks of C-ration beef and steaming rice and a pot of green tea and small brown wafers. Afterwards they lay on the floor bed, watching the embers fade in the brazier until they drifted into sleep.

They woke with the first brightening of the balcony screen, ate a breakfast of scrambled dried eggs and tea, and set off to explore Nikko. They walked down the road away from where they had come, bowing to Japanese passersby, occasionally meeting meandering

American soldiers who looked at him enviously. They came to a steep wooded hillside where rough-hewn stairs ascended and disappeared and they followed them to the top and through an arched *tori*. Looking ahead, they drew in their breaths. They were entering a village of large red-and-gold temples, beautifully wrought and inset with mother-of-pearl and colored glass. "*Jinga*," the girl said, and translated; "Shinto shrine." They toured the interiors, marveling at the multiarmed goddesses and the giant Buddhas that rose almost to the ceilings. Once, murmuring an apology, she left him and stood facing a towering Buddha, her arms held closely to her sides. He saw her lips move as if in prayer, then she bowed stiffly several times, backed away, and returned to him. She looked up timidly, and when he smiled understandingly, she expelled a breath as if in relief that no explanation was necessary. They signed a parchment scroll as evidence of their visit and went silently back down the hillside stairs.

They had a lunch of rice and raw fish (which, surprisingly, he found palatable) and cold Japanese beer at a roadside shack. In the afternoon they took a cable tram to the top of a sheer mountain, where they wandered the streets buying locally crafted souvenirs in the small shops. Later they were directed to the lake, and here found a small secluded cove, allowing them to strip off their clothing and plunge into the cold water. Afterwards they lay in a grassy hollow and made love in the slanting sun.

They arrived back at the hotel at dusk and the maid amazed him with great portions of steaming sukiyaki. "Japanese have black market too," the girl said, pretending a look of smugness.

It went like that for the next three days—a fantasy world where there was no hunger, no desolation, no loneliness, and all was love. When Sunday afternoon came, and it was time to leave for their train, they had a final drink and walked about patting the walls and blessing this house. Then they went reluctantly down the stairs, said their sad farewells, entered the same exploding taxi, and lurched off to the plaintive cries of *Sayonara*.

"Catherine, are you all right?"

It was Helen, calling from just outside the kitchen. Catherine hopped up and went to the door. "Yes," she called, "I'm all right, Helen." She heard the kitchen door swing shut.

She knew it was Helen's way of saying she should start changing into her dress. But there was still plenty of time. Besides, her mother had said something about stopping by after tennis to see some relative of hers from New York. Maybe she would be late.

Catherine closed the door and went back to her father's Japanese story.

San Francisco - Sausalito

1968

IV

Slowly rotating his big shaggy head, Carter Cornman sighted in momentarily on each of the eight men seated at the long conference table. Apparently satisfied that he now held them in thrall, his eyes returned to the red-white-and-blue boxes stacked in front of him. He patted the top box almost with affection.

Here it comes, thought Scott Welles, and slid up more erectly in the leather chair on Cornman's right. The president, he knew, was about to go into his peroration, a supplication that would end the meeting on a note of moral challenge. He was not quite prepared for:

"So I say to each and every one of you, the day you go home from this office without having advanced the success of this product—a revolutionary breakthrough by our biggest client—that day you can consider *wasted!*"

Scott's hand went reflexively to his mouth and he bowed his head. Accustomed as he had long since become to Carter Cornman's doomsday utterances mixed with rah-rah platitudes, this was too much. Could the man possibly be speaking of *spaghetti*, thin sticks of brittle dough? He could—for this was new, now, for-the-first-time-in-history spaghetti: a special additive prevented it from sticking to the bottom of the pan. A milestone in the progress of man, thought Scott. His mind flashed back to President Kennedy's famous inaugural injunction, paraphrasing it only slightly: Ask not what this spaghetti can do for you; ask what *you* can do for this spaghetti! He shot a glance across at Phipps Spain, senior vice president of the agency and supervisor of the account. Spain had molded his usually satirical expression into the look of a man who has ascended to heaven and is facing the twelve apostles.

"I needn't remind you," said Cornman, "that there isn't an advertising agency in San Francisco that wouldn't go all out to get this piece of our client's business. In fact, our client suggested that it might be wise to see what another agency can do. However, I prevailed upon them to give us first crack at it. In such a situation, failure on our part could be catastrophic, jeopardizing our position as agency for every other product in the line." He paused to let the needle plunge to the marrow.

Scott Welles could almost smell the fear in the room. He felt only a vague sadness.

Cornman's solid pink face became almost benign. "Maybe I'm old-fashioned," he said quietly, "but I believe *profoundly* in the adage, 'The team that *won't* be beaten, *can't* be beaten.'" Another pause. "Phipps Spain, of course, will captain this operation, working in close collaboration with me. Scott, I would appreciate it if you, as creative director, would personally call the creative signals. The three of us will have a kickoff meeting in my office at nine A.M. Monday." He stood up, smiling thinly. "That is all."

The department heads silently filed out. Phipps Spain caught up with Scott in the corridor.

"My friend," he said with a look of mock concern, "what do you suppose will happen when the Italian government hears about this revolutionary spaghetti breakthrough?"

"They'll declare war on the United States."

"Exactly. Wow, that Cornman! Norman Vincent Rockne. I could smell the wintergreen, the sweaty armpits, the jockstraps. That what made you grab your mouth?"

"I was stifling a cheer."

Spain massaged his tan cheeks. "I've got to get rid of this business face. Got time for a drink? It's past five. Every ad type in town is already eighty proof."

"Another time, Phipps. I've got a few things to clean up."

"You'll burn yourself out. Okay, we'll have it tomorrow night. I hear we're getting smashed at your house before the club dance."

Remembering, Scott felt an interior grimace. Carter Cornman himself would be there with his subjugated wife, Evelyn. And, later, they'd join the whole cretinous tennis club crowd. Even when the people changed, they seemed the same, all spouting boozy nonsense, casting themselves as unique, fascinating individuals before they were reclaimed once more by the stupefying conformity of their existence. How the hell did Tina stand it? He felt a surge of guilt. She had her reasons—his eyes blinked away the specifics—understandable if not entirely condonable. How did *he* stand it? Probably because he got it in smaller doses. And he had his work, not really quite as absurd as Cornman's pronouncements made it sound. The thought gave him no nourishment, only the awareness, more nagging of late, that what talents he possessed had been dedicated to triviality.

Taking the back stairs to the floor below, he found that everyone had left. As he crossed the open area to his private office, his steps quickened. He had not as yet checked the afternoon mail, having gone directly from a client presentation to the conference room. Perhaps the monthly letter had come.

He found it on his desk, atop a pile of junk mail. He glanced at the name of the sender—G. Takimoto—and the Tokyo postmark; it had been mailed three days ago. He tore open the envelope and read each sentence slowly, pausing occasionally to gaze at the ceiling, forming an image.

Three times he read the letter, then held it over the waste basket and shredded it into little pieces.

The delivery would be made on Saturday. He was struck by an inner tremor. Tokyo time was seventeen hours later—already Saturday, about ten-thirty A.M. Perhaps Tak—George Washington Takimoto—was at this moment sitting cross-legged on the tatami floor of the small house that Scott Welles had not visited in more than twenty years.

He remembered again how he had been nagged by guilt at that time. But Tina, thousands of miles away, had become a blur in his mind. There were only her letters, and the vision they evoked was not pleasant. Catalogues of woe: "The prices are outrageous! I'm cooped up in this God-awful room most of the time! I have to stand in long lines for cigarettes, then settle for something like Sano, my God! I ripped my last pair of nylons and they're almost impossible to get if you want to stay a decent woman!"

He sat there thinking for about ten minutes. The idea that lately had been running through his mind jelled into determination. If what he had planned were to be discovered by Tina, she might, out of wounded pride, leave him. No great tragedy in itself, but it would surely mean that she would take Catherine. But the odds were good that he could manage it so that she would never suspect.

He spun a sheet of paper into his typewriter and rapidly typed a letter to Tak. It should reach him by Monday morning.

V

Gardner Prescott had been living on the boat berthed in Sausalito for a week when, on that late afternoon, he saw the woman approaching. She wore sandals, jaunty lowslung slacks, and a pale blue sweater that bounced jubilantly as she pranced down the wooden stairs to the narrow boardwalk. She came toward him with a swinging, purposeful stride, stopping halfway out and spinning around, tawny hair bannering in the breeze, to review the motley assemblage of floating misfits: reconverted tugs, scows with superimposed A-frame houses, fishing hulks painted in pastel colors, decaying houseboats, even a small, splintered barge on which was bolted a fairly modern mobile home.

They provided a bizarre contrast to the magnificent view of the great bay: San Francisco, beyond the tacking sailboats, rising white on its seven tiered hills; the red south tower of the Golden Gate Bridge starting its leap to the ragged headland hunched high above Gardner's perch on the forward bunkhouse; below, the docks of marinas and restaurants jutting from the curved shore. Little wonder that John Sheckley, the owner of the boat and Gardner's friend since the Korean war, had called it "the sonofabitching living end as a place to create." Since owning it, he had written Gardner, his whole art style had changed—"no more touristy stuff"—and his canvasses were making it with sophisticated buyers.

Gardner, however, had found the scene inspirational to the point of immobility: the new novel had lain untouched for days. He was the too-contented victim, he had decided, of another piece of Sheckley philosophy: "Inside a boat, cradled gently on the deep, there is a sense of isolation from the world's bullshit that is rarely found." That, of course, aside from the boat being offered to him rent-free, had been the ultimate lure. Immediately he had borrowed the flight money from his mother. John Sheckley, with his wife and two children, had thereupon taken off for a six weeks' tour of the South Pacific.

The woman had now come close enough for Gardner to see her delicate jawline, the solid bone structure that stretched her tan skin, the blue eyes that shone incandescently in the rays of the descending sun.

She stopped below him, shaded her eyes, and said, "Excuse me. I'm looking for a Gardner Prescott. Do you know him?"

So he knew she was Bettina Welles.

"Hi, Tina," he said.

Her face broke into a broad white grin, and for an illusory instant she seemed once again the Tina he had known some twenty-four years ago (though her hair hung long now) when he was no more than thirteen or fourteen. (And she was what?—sixteen, seventeen?) He recognized the contradictory mouth—upper lip thin and capable of stiff defiance, lower lip full and glossy like a bite of ripe exotic fruit. Her cheeks and longish nose crinkled in the remembered way when she smiled, as if she were breathing in a delightful fragrance. But now the crinkles were deeper.

"Gard! Can that gorgeous man sitting up there really be Gardner Prescott? I don't believe it!"

"Come aboard. I'll show you the birthmark on my hip."

She nodded reminiscently and with mock resignation. "Yes, it's you all right, fresh as ever"—and she started around the prow, bold-breasted and confident.

She was some sort of distant cousin on his mother's

side, and he and his older brother had spent two summers with her on the farm of a great aunt in Pennsylvania. They had picked apples together, ridden the penned pigs, fed the chickens, raced with tender bare feet across stubbled fields, had rotten-egg fights in the barn. And she had taught him to dance. He could still hear the tinny sound of the portable phonograph playing on the rose-scented side porch, hear the floorboards creak as they slid and swayed to a sultry big-band arrangement of "Mood Indigo," cheeks and bodies glued together in the fashion of the time. Once, in the darkness, her thigh rigidly between his legs, their mouths had touched and she electrified him by flicking his lips with the tip of her tongue.

Another time—a Sunday, and the farm swarming with kin—they had played hide and seek. Tina had grabbed his hand and dashed him into a stand of trees beyond the apple orchard. They had hidden in a leaf-lined hollow surrounded by thick bushes. She had hugged him close to her as if—at least so he thought at the time—to shrink them out of sight. His face was hot and his heart clamored and before he knew it his hand was on her breast. He saw the corner of her mouth curl into a little smile and she leaned back on her hands and let him play with her. They had gone there often after that and soon his hands were slipping inside the top of her blouse investigating firm, bra-less flesh.

He had gone no further than that, fearful that perhaps she was indulging him more from boredom than desire. Still, he remembered her saying after that last summer, when they were all about to leave for home, "Gardner Prescott, when you grow up you're going to be a heart-breaker." Well, at thirty-eight he had been long grown up and had broken no hearts, but had chipped his own, over a wife who had left him for a new-rich stock speculator. Since that experience he'd had little time or inclination for anything but transient relationships. He had been too busy learning to become a writer.

He scrambled down to the small deck in the stern as Tina came along the walkway on the port side.

"No ladder, no gate on this bucket," he said, looking down at her. "You've got to slide under the railing."

She grinned at the challenge and held up her hands. He grasped her wrists, surprised at their strength, and hauled her up until her feet firmed on the edge of the deck. Then she grabbed hold of the lower white steel railing, squatted, and slid her long legs gracefully under. Her beautifully packaged rump grazed the deck surface and he stood there admiring it, forgetting to give her a hand. But he recovered in time to help her to her feet.

Facing her in the bright sunlight, he could see the tiny lines fanning out from the corners of her eyes, the deep parentheses formed by her smile, and noted the blue chiffon scarf masking her throat. With mild shock, he realized that she must be past forty. But judging by the overall look of her—the clear, taut skin, the firm, almost girlish body maneuvered with supple grace—she was giving time one hell of a fight.

She dug a pack of cigarettes from the pocket of her slacks, lit one, cupping the match in strong hands, and puffed furiously. "Damn you, Gard," she said, "you've been here a whole week and haven't so much as phoned." She pointed her cigarette beyond the long row of anchored boats, beyond the tackle shops and marine showrooms, and, behind them, squatters' huts built of scrap lumber and galvanized metal, up to the rolling hills that rimmed the town. "And us living right up there."

"I know. I've been stuck on chapter four. I was going to call you this week."

"You'd have had to hurry. Today is Friday."

That surprised him. Time had slipped meaninglessly away while he had been playing God to his fantasies, adjusting ghostly lives to suit fictional purposes. The interior world had become for him more real than the actual one and a lot more comfortable.

"Mother write you?" He imagined his widowed mother sitting alone in her New York apartment, fretting about her son some three thousand miles away on a strange boat; finally dashing off a note to Bettina Welles in the hope of recruiting her as a maternal surrogate.

"Yes," Tina said, "I got the letter yesterday. I'm supposed to keep an eye on you." She clasped her hands lightly around his neck, raised her face and brushed a kiss on his cheek, then arched back and studied his face. "And you're very pleasant to the eye, my lad. Tall, thick black hair, deep-set eyes, and a nice chin. Heavens, how have you managed to stay single?"

"I was married for almost three years. She was allergic to poverty, so it bombed."

"Yes, I'd forgotten. I heard about that from someone."

He wondered what she had heard. Certainly not that his wife had taken sadistic pleasure in diminishing him. Remembering her shrill, ranting voice, he felt again the old pain and the deep, unrealized need for self-assertion.

"Since then I've been having a secret affair with a cute little Remington."

She leaned back against the railing, puffed on her cigarette until it almost singed her lips, then flipped it over the side. "Hardly a secret affair. I read your novel." Her expression turned grave and he remembered how, even as a girl, her moods would swing swiftly from joy to depression; the elastic mouth that could smile so readily could also sulk. "Oh Gard, it's *good*."

"You're one of a very small minority," he said. "Of course, a very *discriminating* minority."

Her eyes blinked rapidly. "How I wish I could do something *creative*," she said wistfully.

"Well, you've got a daughter. That's creative."

"Yes," she said shortly, "I've got a daughter."

He remembered then that her daughter was adopted. "Is she a nice child?" he asked gently.

"Oh, Catherine's a lovely child." She lit another cigarette and stared abstractedly at the orange tip. It was as though she were suddenly alone.

He changed the subject. "And you've got a creative husband. He's in advertising, isn't he?"

She gave her head a shake, flinging out her shoulder-length hair. Her smile returned; this time faintly mocking. "Very big in advertising," she said. "Vice president and creative director in the San Francisco office of one of those monstrous Madison Avenue ad factories."

"You sound disapproving."

"Oh, I approve of it—especially the money. But from what I hear, it sounds like something Fred Allen once said about radio vice presidents: Promptly at nine A.M. an office boy places a molehill on each vice president's desk. He has until five o'clock to make it into a mountain."

He had heard the line, but laughed.

"Scott's getting to feel that way about it. 'The mouse race,' he said the other day. Once, a long time ago, he wanted to write novels too. Serious things about how people survive in a harsh society. But after he got out of the army he had to think about our own survival. So he took a job in advertising. He was good at it and it wasn't too long before gobs of money started rolling in." She shrugged. "His dream got buried by success."

"There's still time," he said. "He must be fairly young."

"He's well past forty." She pronounced the number as if it were the code word for oblivion.

He smiled. "As I said, still young."

She patted his shoulder appreciatively. "Aren't you nice."

She clamped the cigarette in her mouth and turned her head away. A sharp wind gusted off the water, sending her hair flying.

"I'm a lousy host," he said, "keeping you standing here. Come below and I'll give you the fifty-cent tour."

In fact, the boat would have warranted an admission charge. In its uniquely elegant way it was as strange as anything afloat in that crazy marina. A thirty-six-foot LCVP (landing craft vehicles and personnel) built by Higgins in the early days of World War Two, it had known the vomiting fear of countless G.I.s chugged ashore in the embattled islands of the South Pacific. Buying it as surplus for four hundred dollars, John Sheckley had added a superstructure of white-painted plywood that gave it the appearance of an aspiring yacht.

Below, down three short stairs, green carpeting covered the deck of the small salon. The bright blue bulkheads were hung with a wild variety of pictures and objects—a faded print of Abraham Lincoln, a Civil War sword, treasure maps, a spiked German helmet, the blueprints of the original boat, some offbeat prints. A picture window faced the aft deck and below it was a built-in couch heaped with multicolored pillows. Another built-in couch, covered in rough-textured saffron material, faced a teak coffee table and two undersized rattan drum chairs. Forward, past the head with its hand-pump toilet and drizzling shower, and through a narrow door, two red-upholstered bunks curved into the prow.

"My God," Tina said, "this must be what Onassis played with when he was a kid."

He told her about John Sheckley and his transformation of the boat. "When we were in Korea together he used to say he'd someday own a yacht. And damned if he didn't make the dream come true. With some compromises, of course."

They were standing in the forward section between the curving red bunks. Tina dropped down on one. He snapped on a record player, stacked with old 78s, that was fitted into the prow. In a moment the soft strains of "Long Ago and Far Away" filled the cabin, with Frankie Carle oozing out the vocal.

He said, "The title of the song selected for your listening pleasure is pure coincidence."

She covered her eyes. "Oh, this is too much."

"Also," he said, "the sun is now almost over the yardarm." He looked at his watch. "It's now quarter to five. We'll cheat. A vodka martini is the best I can offer."

Lights appeared in her eyes. "A vodka martini would be dandy. A pitcher of them would be heaven."

"I just happen to have a pitcher."

VI

She remained seated—pondering something, he thought—while he ducked into the main cabin and mixed the martinis at the tiny sink. Coming back, he poured the drinks, set the frosted pitcher on the floor, and perched on the bunk opposite her.

They drank silently, hearing the muffled squawks of gulls, and the soft slap of waves against the hull. Tina took quick gulps, gripping hard on the glass, smoking as if she couldn't wait to experience lung cancer. He poured her another drink and began cautiously reminiscing about the summer days on the farm. She smiled and nodded at intervals and put in a word here and there, but she seemed preoccupied.

Suddenly, midway through her third drink, which she had poured, she said, "I liked you so much, Gard, even though you were barely in your teens. How often I wished then that you were older." She contemplated her glass. "Do you remember our hideout in the woods?"

He had deliberately omitted that. "Sure," he said easily. "That's where I used to brag about becoming a great writer."

Her eyes flashed boldly into his. "You also did other things. You were very—*advanced*."

He was startled. Her tone was nostalgic rather than teasing.

"I remember," he said, falsely casual. "Gardner Prescott—dedicated sex fiend, junior grade."

She downed her drink, poured another, crossed over and sat beside him. "Oh God," she burst out, "I'm so damned unhappy."

So now it seemed clear, and it was all so ordinary. She and her husband weren't making it. Scott Welles, entering middle age, perhaps panicky that life was slipping away, perhaps feeling the hot breath of corporate youth on his neck, had become an all-around bastard to live with.

"Can I help?" he said.

She was silent, bending to the ashtray on the floor and slowly grinding out her cigarette. When she sat back, she cradled her head on his shoulder. He could smell the scent drifting from her mass of tawny hair, and, glancing down, see her breasts swelling the blue sweater. Something quaked and rose in him and he knew, with a pang of regret, that no longer was she simply a relative seeking the comfort of fond memories, but a woman eager to be intimately discovered.

Her hand scratched like a nervous claw at his inner thigh. He imagined her anguished loneliness.

She raised and turned her face, her lips unavoidably grazing his. Then they were kissing, her mouth moist and ravenous. He thought of her husband, whom he now would probably never meet, and pictured him drunk and abusive.

The voice of Kenny Sargent was singing "Green Eyes." ...

Her hand moved from his thigh and he heard the metallic whisper of a zipper. Then, somehow, alternately standing and sitting, the kissing never stopping, she peeled off her slacks, stripped off her sweater, flung aside her bra, and stood squirming against him in lavender-lace panties as she fumbled with the buttons of his shirt. His hands climbed the gently curved ladder of her ribs. He thought of nothing.

They used both bunks. They used the floor. In the gray light, they sat, kneeled, crouched, rolled, flexed, thrashed—ended up stretched on the green carpeting, a shaft of sunlight splitting the closed curtain of a high window and striking his back. Her mouth, next to his ear, breathed the last of a keening wail.

They sat up, damp and exhausted, and leaned back against the edge of a bunk. She reached for her tangled slacks, fished out the crumpled pack of cigarettes, and lit one for each of them. Taking deep drags, she poured two watery martinis and handed him one. Her face had relaxed into an expression of exquisite relief, and she smiled lazily into his eyes through a cloud of swirling smoke.

"You see? You see how I always wanted you?"

He felt a stirring of remorse, but said, "Hurricane Tina. Damned near blew us out of the water."

"You mean I was exciting?" She said it ingenuously, as if she *really* wondered.

"Like wow!"

Arms resting across her flat stomach, she smiled a secret smile, her full lower lip clasped contentedly over the thin upper one. She had stopped puffing the cigarette and the ash grew long as she gazed vacantly into space. He was thinking about her husband and her daughter and wondering just what the hell he had gotten into. . . .

Her cigarette ash dropped, stinging the delicate white skin next to her pubic hair, and her arms jerked from her stomach as she slapped at the shattered ashes.

For the first time, he saw the scar. It was thin, pale, and herringbone-stitched, running straight down from her navel and disappearing into the V-shaped patch.

She swore. Sucking in air, she darted a glance at him, aware of what had attracted his eyes. She frowned, eyes blinking, and quickly hugged her stomach. There was an enormous pause. He concentrated on his martini, looking straight ahead at the opposite red bunk.

"Just one of life's little accidents," she said bitterly.

One drink later, dressed and facing each other on the rattan chairs in the main cabin, the record player silenced, she told him about herself and Scott Welles.

She had been a sophomore and he a senior in the same high school when they first met. They had dated a number of times but limited their intimacies to "a few chaste, Life Saver Kisses, I was ready to tear my clothes off, but I guess Scott was afraid I'd go stiff as a door and slam it shut. He seemed happy enough that I was a good dancer and laughed a lot."

Right after Scott graduated, his father died suddenly of a coronary and he moved with his mother and brother to a two-family house on the outskirts of Sacramento. All three of them went to work and he didn't see Tina again for a number of years. When he did—running into her one Saturday morning in a department store—it was as though they had been banking their fires waiting for that moment to erupt. She lived with a girl friend—her parents had been divorced and gone East—and that night, her roommate away overnight, Scott visited her apartment and stayed through breakfast. Nostalgia for all the carefree, vanished days when they were part of an elite high school group had been catalyst enough to scatter clothes to the floor and by morning bring them to the solemn conclusion that they were passionately in love.

Tina had married Scott Welles shortly before his induction into the army. For months he had been shuttled about the country, seeing her only on brief, sporadic leaves spent mostly in the bedrooms and bars of jammed motels. His assignment to Japan had been accepted by both of them with something like relief, a welcome hiatus to what under the circumstances had become a burdensome marriage. When he returned, more than a year later, they determined to settle down and have a child. For about three years, during which "sex became like something conducted in a laboratory," nothing happened. Fulfillment, it appeared, would have to be found in other pursuits.

"Scott found his in business," she said. "I went the tennis club route." She smiled sardonically. "It was a thoroughly contemporary marriage, unexciting but comfortably organized."

So completely had they adjusted to remaining childless that when Tina finally became pregnant, they were more stunned than enthralled. But soon they responded conventionally and became as fatuous as the expectant parents in the situation comedies that crowded the television screens.

Complications occurred during labor and the baby was removed by Caesarean section.

"Thus my fancy needlework," Tina said.

"But—"

"The baby never made it," she said shortly. "The cause of death had a very impressive name—Down's Syndrome." She tossed her long hair. "Let's forget it."

She got up, went to the sink, and splashed straight vodka into her glass. She stood, sipping, looking down into his eyes. "At least the docs didn't take away my womanhood," she said with some defiance.

He smiled, feeling an odd emphathy. "You're more than enough woman for any man, Tina."

Her face brightened. "I hoped you'd say something like that." She sat down, taking quick puffs of the inevitable cigarette. In a low, throaty voice she said, "I was terribly depressed for a long time. Scott tried to help, maybe tried *too* hard—it showed. He took me to the theater, on picnics, on trips, even joined me at the club—not the one we belong to now—which I knew he detested. Then, on the *Lurline* going to Hawaii, we met the Pawlings—Mary and Tom and their daughter Catherine. We got to be close friends—they lived near us down on the Peninsula—and we saw each other just about every week after we got home." She paused, gulping the last of her drink. "Then, a long time later, came that terrible, terrible day—*two* terrible days."

He half closed his eyes as Tina continued the story, the events forming in his mind like scenes in a novel.

A late Sunday afternoon. The Pawlings driving up Highway 101 from a weekend in Monterey. An oncoming car jumping the divider strip, crashing head-on into the Pawlings' big Imperial. Tom killed instantly. Mary and little Catherine rushed in a screaming ambulance to the hospital.

The next day, Monday. Scott and Tina at Mary Pawling's bedside. Tina's eyes acquisitive even while she protested the words whispered by Catherine's dying mother.

"If I go, I want her to be yours," said Mary Pawling. "I know Tom would agree. You've been our best friends. And there's no one else."

"You're going to be fine," Tina said.

"Will you take her? Please tell me you'll take her."

"You mustn't even think like that, Mary."

"We'll take her," Scott said.

"Thank you. I'll arrange for it today."

That evening, an hour after the lawyer had left, Mary Pawling joined her husband in death. Catherine lay in an adjoining room, head swathed in bandages but her life unthreatened.

In Catherine they had seen not only an object of love, but also a catalyst that hopefully would energize their marriage.

"It didn't work out that way," Tina said drearily. She dipped her head and massaged between her eyes.

"It was a big"—her hand pulled away and she groped for the word—"disappointment."

"You mean Catherine drove you and Scott further apart?"

She considered for a moment, "Yes, that was the result."

"Why?" he asked gently. "Because you competed for her affection? I've heard of that happening."

"It wasn't a question of competition," she said cryptically. "Let's not talk about it."

Why the evasion, he wondered. Had Tina begun to develop an unconscious resentment of Catherine from the very beginning—because she was not her own child, because she was a constant reminder of the one Tina had lost?

"It's time I got home," Tina said. "Will you come tomorrow for cocktails and dinner?"

"That doesn't sound too smart, Tina. After what you and I—"

"Please. Scott knows you're here and wants to meet you. You'll have to do it some time." She smiled and stroked his cheek. "Relax, darling. And don't feel any guilt. Not ever. Whatever we want to be to each other will be completely justified."

Tokyo

1947

VII

Catherine had not moved on the bed, except to turn the pages of "Notes for a Novel" and frequently raise her head for long periods of reverie. She saw now that she was coming to the end and she forced herself to read even more slowly than before. . . .

On a bitterly cold day in early January, the American got the order that would return him to the United States for discharge. He had been expecting it for a long time, preparing himself for the sorrow of separation by consciously evoking memories of American streets showered with lights, stores packed with goods, a great shimmering bay abob with boats, fine civilian clothes, crisp white sheets—a land untouched by the fury of dropping bombs.

But all these thoughts were overpowered by the knowledge of what must now be forsaken—an adoring, selfless girl, a loving family, a small square room covered with straw mats, a battered desk, a pitiful vegetable garden.

He waited until after they had finished dinner and were sipping whiskey before he told her that he would be gone within three days. Her reaction startled him.

She smiled.

It was a smile he could not fathom until she said, "Please, you don't be sad. Three days. A long time." Then he realized that she too had been preparing for this moment, concerned more with his feelings than with her own. He clutched her to him, unable to speak for the thickness in his throat.

She said, "We will not tell family. Until after."

It was a cruel time to be leaving. Twice during the harsh winter she had become sick. But not so seriously that she had to be hospitalized. Her temperature had hovered around 100 degrees and she had occasionally been nauseated, but in both instances she had responded favorably to the ministrations of the goateed doctor. The old gentleman had touched him reassuringly on the shoulder and said not to worry—just a germ—but his eyes behind the horn-rimmed glasses had examined his face inquiringly, as if questioning that this former foe could be so deeply concerned about the welfare of one Nipponese girl. He urged himself not to worry about her—she had lost no weight, in fact seemed to have gained a few pounds, and although her face appeared drawn, she was charged with energy. But he worried.

Two days later he was alerted to report for processing within twenty-four hours at the Point of Embarkation base in Yama, just outside of Yokohama. That night, his last, the girl gave him a party at her parents' house, although she had not told them the reason for it. Brother greeted them at the door dressed only in dyed-black long-johns, which they all thought was hilariously funny. Mama-san wore her usual kimono, but she had topped her head with a knitted army cap, as black now as her hair. Papa-san was wrapped in a G.I. sweater, also black. Sister stood in the corner proudly holding the hand of her grinning child, now able to stand, whose head was skinned into the white bonnet he had bought her so long ago.

An old portable record player that Brother had dug up from somewhere gave out the tiny strains of "Slow Boat to China." The table and a section of the floor were spread with food, partly the rations he had heaped upon the family, but, more abundantly, rice and fish and odd seafood he could not identify (nor did he want to after nibbling a tasty snack and learning it was dried and salted fish eyes). They ate hugely, washing the food down with a gallon or so of sake. Dessert was provided by Brother, who disappeared and returned with paper cones of crushed ice drenched with red syrup. They switched to the whiskey, and after a while the family, as if sensing the finality of the occasion, insisted that he go through all his jokes and imitation routines. It was after three when he and the girl left on a wave of laughter and good wishes, Papa-san unsoberly avowing that the American was truly a great man—"No Boolshit."

In bed, they stayed awake until dawn, doing deliberately all the things that had given them so much pleasure, as if to etch each gesture forever on their minds. There were sighs but no tears and never a mention of parting. They slept for two hours, awakening to celebrate each other for one more time, and then dressed and took their last walk together up the dirt road, now frozen solid, to the El station. They stood at the foot of the stone stairs, whipped by the wind, holding each other tightly, not speaking, their breaths in the frigid air forming an aura around their joined faces. Then they heard the distant clatter of the train and he broke away.

From the platform, the train roaring in, he looked down and saw her, waving, her lips moving repeatedly to form the word he knew too sadly and too well: *Sayonara*. He gazed beyond her and saw, in the curve of the road, the erect, undaunted figure of Mama-san, arm waving. The girl would not have to go home alone.

He entered the G.I. car and heard the door bang behind him.

At two o'clock the next afternoon he was notified

that his orders had been postponed for a day. He felt a surge of exhilaration. One more night with the girl he thought he had left forever. But thinking about it, imagining it in all its intimate detail, he began to have doubts. Could he submit her—or himself—to the ordeal of another parting? It was over, relinquished bravely and with grace. Painfully he decided against it.

But that evening, drinking with his nisei friend at a bar, he became overwhelmed with longing. Once more, just once more before they were separated irrevocably by an ocean and it all became a lost dream. He left his friend and in a trancelike state walked to Tokyo station and caught a train.

Starlight flashed on the icy stones in the dirt road as he hurried toward the distant cluster of houses. Passing her parents' house, he saw that the single bulb was lit, but when he reached the other, the one they had shared, he found it in darkness. Probably she had sought the solace of her family.

He retraced his steps and stood in the empty street before her parents' house watching an occasional shadow pass behind the rice paper. He recognized the silhouettes of Mama-san and Papa-san and Brother, but the beloved shape he yearned to see did not appear. Without thinking, he walked silently along the side of the house toward the vegetable garden. At the corner he stopped abruptly and gripped the slick bamboo support. She was standing at the edge of the garden, almost facing him, gazing up at the sky.

Her arms were folded across her breasts, as if to cradle some precious emotion. She was as rigidly still as a wax doll, chin raised, high cheekbones glinting under the light of the stars. He started to take a step forward, then checked himself as she suddenly performed a reminiscent ritual: her arms dropped to her sides and she bowed stiffly three times, just as she had done when confronting the great Buddha in Nikko.

He backed off, knowing at that instant that he could not violate the peace she was supplicating from her ancestral gods.

He slumped back up the dirt road, the tears in his eyes shattering the speeding headlight beam of an approaching train. He started to run.

Sausalito

1968

VIII

"Catherine! Just what are you doing in those clothes!"

Heart leaping, the Japanese reverie blasted, Catherine whirled to a sitting position and faced her mother. Tina Welles stood with one hand knuckled on the doorknob, the other gripping a cigarette. Her eyes were dark with anger, tan skin crimson.

"Why, I . . ." Catherine stopped, seeing than an explanation had suddenly become unnecessary. Tina was now staring beyond her, at the bedspread.

"What's this you've got?" She strode into the room and stood over the bed. Catherine slid up toward the pillow and scooped up her grinning tiger, wrapping him in her arms. She didn't answer.

Tina bent toward the bedspread, her thick, tawny hair falling forward, masking her face. "Pictures of Japan," she said in a puzzled voice. She bent closer. "And something your father wrote." She contemplated the litter silently for a moment, then turned away.

Catherine saw her mother's back tense, saw puffs of cigarette smoke billow out and shatter against the flowered wallpaper. She hugged the tiger more tightly as her mother swung around.

This time Tina's voice was almost gentle, coaxing. "Where did you find them, Catherine?"

"Well, the door . . . the door was open. So I went inside and—"

"The door? *What* door?"

Catherine said miserably, "The door to the storage closet."

"The *storage* closet! Catherine, I told you never . . ." Tina jammed the cigarette between her full lips, as if to plug the stridency of her tone. Smoke jetted from her mouth and nose as she willed herself to say quietly, "Just *where* in the storage closet, Catherine?"

Haltingly, eyes shifting to her reclining lion, Catherine told her.

"I see." Then, to herself, "A footlocker"—as if she had never heard of it. Cigarette jutting from her lips, she leaned down, pushed the pictures and papers into a pile, and snapped them up. She started toward the door, then turned, pointing a nicotined finger. "As for you, young lady, you will stay in your room."

Alone behind the closed door, Catherine wondered why her mother had not been more severe. And why she had not said another word about the jeans and T-shirt.

Nevertheless she went to her closet and took down the short pale green dress she had worn that morning.

In her bedroom, skinning out of her slacks, Tina wondered why she should be so upset. The manuscript caused no concern: she had flipped randomly through it, concluding quickly that it was merely the immature ramblings of a then-aspiring author. She had hidden it in a drawer beneath her lingerie, perhaps to peruse at some future time.

The pictures were another matter. They reeked of adultery—first sensed intuitively, then graphically reinforced by the adoration glowing from those slanted eyes peering up from the glossy prints on her bed. A cute little thing, nothing more, she thought scornfully. Probably bought for a bar of chocolate and a few cigarettes. Tina had read such stories in the newspapers, never thinking to associate them with the man who had then been her husband for perhaps a year. Incredible, she would have thought, that Scott Welles was shacking up with a Japanese slut while his wife was surviving on allotment checks and a pittance from her father. Barely enough, she recalled, to spare her from some dismal job. But God, that awful one-room dungeon in south San Francisco! Was that what was disturbing her? Self-pity, outraged righteousness, after all these years of placid estrangement? No, it was something else. Catherine!

Even though Catherine's young mind may not have grasped it, the pictures had made her a witness to Tina's past humiliation. A *pleased* witness, Tina thought. No sympathy for her mother—oh no, never. More likely delight that her father had experienced something so exotically romantic.

What *about* Scott—how should she handle this discovery with him? Show him the pictures and dismiss them casually, as if they had no illicit significance? Or return everything to the foot-locker and say nothing?

She considered it as she stood naked, smoking a cigarette, staring down at the picture of her youthful husband, equally naked. The great Scott Welles, respected by his associates for his integrity, his contempt for hypocrisy—revealed now as both a cheat and a hypocrite. No one, of course, so long after the event, would view it that way, except Scott himself. But that was enough. Enough perhaps to make him abdicate his role of moral judge where she was concerned. Not that he ever *said* anything. But the judgment was there—in his remoteness, his preoccupation with business, his permissiveness with Catherine—an implicit rebuke to Tina's own methods of discipline.

If Scott became aware that she knew of his youthful transgression, wouldn't that tend to equalize their relationship, freeing her from the remorse that sometimes inhibited her own independent life style? Yes.

Oddly she felt no remorse whatsoever about the tempestuous interlude she had just shared with Gardner. Perhaps because she had wanted nothing from him, a penniless writer, except of course affection and understanding and, above all, she conceded, a reassurance that she was still desirable. *That* he had certainly given her. She thought back fondly to the early Gardner Prescott, only a boy, who, in a leafy hollow, had made his tentative bated-breath assaults on her breasts. Long after, she had often regretted that she had not seized the opportunity to go much further. She shook off the memory and went into the stall shower.

She dressed with great care, even though they were staying home. For once she would be satisfied to be alone with her husband.

Going downstairs, the pictures tucked into the single pocket of her yellow shift, she was glad to see Helen preparing to leave. Now she could drink unobserved and plan her approach to Scott.

IX

As soon as she greeted him at the door he asked where Catherine was.

"In her room," Tina said mildly. "She's being punished."

His eyelids flickered. "What was it this time?"

Tina smiled tolerantly. "Nothing serious really. You know Catherine. She's always getting into things she shouldn't."

"Yes." The sympathy in his eyes, Tina knew, was for his daughter, not his wife.

"I've got martinis set up on the deck. It's a beautiful evening."

He looked at her curiously, then followed her across the large, beam-ceilinged living room and through the open glass doors. They sat on broad padded divans facing a deep, narrow valley that snaked through forested hills. It was nearing seven o'clock and the sun was slipping behind a distant escarpment. Below it, a scattering of lights blinked through the trees that lay in shadow. Tina poured the martinis from a frosted glass pitcher and they lounged back, Scott looking somewhat uncomfortable; usually upon arriving, he hid immediately behind the evening paper.

She waited until they had half emptied their glasses before saying, "I came across something today that should interest you."

His taut face, as he turned it to her in the sunlight, became attentive, blue eyes steady, full mouth curving in an inquiring half-smile. The impression conveyed was one of easy confidence, as though he were a man who without arrogance had satisfactorily made most of life's important decisions. He was, Tina thought, unconsciously assuming the carefully contrived image employed to impress advertising clients. She felt a sudden impatience.

She slid the pictures from her pocket and handed them to him. "Some scenes," she said casually, "of Scott Welles serving his country."

There was tension in his grasp and his eyes turned to blue slate as he contemplated the first picture—Sinjuko cooking over the floor grate. "Well," he said with only a hint of surprise, the half-smile frozen on his face. He fanned them out like a hand of cards. The smile began to melt.

Tina lit a cigarette. "You wrote some things on the back," she said helpfully.

He went through them without comment or expression, not looking up, turning each snapshot to read the inscription. Finishing, he dropped the stack carelessly on the round redwood table. "Through darkest Japan with gun and camera," he said easily. "I thought I'd forgotten them."

"The pictures or the people?"

He sipped his drink. "Oh I remember the people. A wonderful family." He paused. "They were friends of Tak's." He looked at her. "I told you about Tak. George Washington Takimoto—the nisei interpreter who worked with me on that army magazine, *Maptalk*."

"But you never told me about the Japanese . . . *family*."

"Didn't I? I thought I had." He reached for the pitcher, refilled their glasses, then lit a cigarette with thoughtful deliberation. "Tak was quite a guy. He was in love with a Japanese girl—perhaps I told you."

He had, several times, long ago. "The girl in the pictures—Sinjuko?"

Scott shifted on the divan. "No. Tak's girl was a bit older. He wanted like hell to marry her, but that was against regulations, let alone bringing her home. I think it was about the middle of forty-seven before our government got civilized and allowed G.I.s to marry Japanese nationals and bring them to the states. Before that, there was only one solution. You got your discharge, then reenlisted, which meant you could choose where you wanted to be assigned. Or, if you had some kind of critically needed specialty—interpreter, say—you could return to Japan as a civilian worker. That's what Tak did—went home to Salinas, then bounced back to Tokyo. He's got a Japanese wife he still adores and three fine kids."

The man, thought Tina, has become positively garrulous. Anything to avoid the subject that burned in both their minds. Well, let him play it out; in a perverse way, she was enjoying the game.

"You sound like you hear from him," she said.

"A few times, over the years."

"I don't recall you mentioning it."

"Maybe I didn't. It wasn't exactly important."

Tina lit another cigarette from the stub of the old one. "I wonder why he didn't bring his wife over here."

She saw his face tighten, as if some inner hostility was struggling to surface. "Why should he? He's got a much better job than he could hope for in this country. Here he might have had to settle for busboy or yard worker. Over there, people respect him and he respects himself. More importantly, why should he drag a Japanese wife over here where she'd have been a second-class citizen, treated with condescension if not contempt?"

She remembered reading an article in a popular magazine that had told of Japanese war brides trying desperately to adjust to life in the United States, often in vain. If the situation had been otherwise, would Scott have abandoned her for Sinjuko? A fantastic thought, but less so when she considered their own aborted wartime marriage. When he had been shipped to Japan, he was somehow not yet a husband, nor she a wife.

Scott had stood up, the pictures wrapped in his hand as if to conceal them. He rubbed briskly at his shoulder. "Getting chilly. I'll go see Catherine. She must have served her sentence by now." He picked up the martini pitcher. "Will you take the glasses?"

So he thought he'd escape. Oh no, my boy. She snatched up the glasses and preceded him inside. As he bent to set the pitcher on the table in front of the long gold sofa, she said, "Wouldn't you like to know where I found them—the pictures?"

He had to have wondered, she thought, but was wary of asking. Suspicion that he was being baited prickled his voice as he said, "Yes, where?"—and his eyes studied her ingenuous smile.

Elaborately she poured another drink, letting his stand there. "Actually, *I* didn't find them. Catherine did." She pushed his glass at him and he took it. "She found them in the storage closet in that footlocker you brought back from Japan." She sat in a green lounge chair, facing the sofa, puffing on a fresh cigarette.

"The footlocker," he said, and seemed to stiffen. "I figured that had been left behind during one of our many moves. God knows, we've lived in enough houses."

"Let's not bring *that* up. The fact is, the footlocker's upstairs and those pictures were in it." Instantly she regretted her tone. She had planned to be very calm, very worldly about it all, letting him make his own bed of thorns.

He sat on the sofa, leaning forward, arms resting on his thighs. "Is that why Catherine's being punished?"

"Yes. I've told her a hundred times to stay out of that closet."

Was that the reason? Or because she found the pictures?

"She deliberately disobeyed me. *That's* the reason. Though I can't say I exactly enjoyed seeing her gloating over those pictures."

"Gloating? Now what makes you think of that word?"

To hell with the way she had planned it. "Because it's the *right* word. She was gloating over the fact that you'd evidently been cheating on me!"

She had expected indignation, not the sudden compassion that softened his eyes. He was condescending to her, tacitly indicating that he understood the true source of her outburst and was sympathetic. Damn him! She gave him a stony stare.

"That's undeserved, Tina," he said quietly. "I don't think such a thought could ever enter Catherine's mind."

"Oh no?" She flung an arm toward the built-in, floor-to-ceiling bookcase. "You don't know how many times I've caught her sneaking into some of our . . . our more *advanced* literature."

His mouth tightened. "Good. Sounds healthy."

Tina gulped her drink and poured herself another.

"But I still don't think the thought occurred to her, Tina. Only to you."

"Well why for God's sake wouldn't it? Not one picture of any of your buddy-buddies. Just that Japanese . . ."

"Is that so remarkable?" he said, the half-smile returning. "I was *in* Japan. It may sound damned strange, but there were a lot of Japanese in Japan."

"That Japanese *girl*. The one who snapped a picture of you stark naked. The one who looked back at you like you were the Emperor himself."

"*All* Japanese girls looked at men like that if they found them likable. Especially American men." Ironically he added, "We were the honorable conquerors."

"She looked conquered all right." She gave a short laugh. "That just-laid look."

"Come off it, Tina. You're making a big deal out of nothing. Besides, the statute of limitations should have run out by now."

"There's no statute of limitations on deceit," she said, but felt defeated.

He regarded her wearily, setting down his glass. "I'm afraid I can't do anything about your imaginings."

She made a last brave try. "Imaginings? Then answer me this: Were you sleeping with that girl or not?"

He pushed to his feet. "Tina, I slept with every woman in Tokyo. MacArthur's orders. Part of our mission to spread democracy."

"You won't give me an answer?"

"Not when you're being so damned ridiculous."

He was right—the way she had handled it *was* ridiculous. She had acted like a bumbling, overzealous prosecutor, making Scott's recalcitrance seem less an evasion of guilt than a rebellion against petty harassment. Still, she was positive that he and the girl had been lovers. Did it matter now? Yes, now of all times she needed some form of moral leverage. She lapsed into a sulky silence.

"It's been a long day," he said, stretching. "I'm going up to take a shower."

She could not resist a parting shot: "I'm afraid there's no oak bucket, soldier. So sorry."

He walked away as though he hadn't heard.

Catherine rose quickly from her crouched position at the head of the stairs. Earlier she had stood there, about to go down, sure of her father's warm protection, when she heard her mother say something about the pictures—say it in a tone she always used when about to burst into anger.

Feeling guilty but unable to budge, Catherine had listened to every word.

When her father reached the landing, she was back in her room, door closed.

She was not shocked by what her mother had said. Only a little frightened, as she herself was when accused of doing something dreadful. But, so far as she could see, her father had done nothing dreadful. She knew he had been sweet and kind to that beautiful Japanese girl, and she to him. What difference could it make to her mother, who had been an ocean away? Supposing he *had* slept with the girl, why get so angry about it *now*, especially when her parents had separate beds and generally acted like they didn't know each other very well? Oh, she knew what "sleeping with" meant; her mother had been right about her sneaking into those books! She had been sort of mixed up at first—the way the people made love had sounded scary. But the more she found out about it, the more right it seemed. It was such a *natural* way, such a wonderful way, to show how much you cared for someone.

The thought became a sudden blush in her mind when her father knocked and looked in—as if he could see right into her brain.

"Hi, prisoner," he said. "I just called the Governor. He agreed to grant you a parole."

She sat up, stifling a giggle with her hand. "Hi. I'm sorry about what I did."

He closed the door behind him. "The whole truth and nothing but the truth—are you *really* sorry?"

She considered her crime. "I'm sorry I disobeyed Mother. I'm sorry I opened your footlocker."

"Breaking and entering. Very serious. The law calls it a felony."

"But I can't say I'm sorry about finding those pictures." She smiled impishly. "I guess you shouldn't tell that to the Governor."

"Never. You'd go right back into the slammer for sure." He came and kissed her cheek and gave her flaxen hair a pat.

"When I go to bed tonight," she said, "will you tell me about Japan?"

"Again? I thought I was boring you. All right, but it will be short. I've got to close myself in the study and do some work. Now, how about coming downstairs?"

"A couple of minutes—after I go to the bathroom."

He gave her hand a squeeze and left.

She did not need to go to the bathroom, but she did need time to think. Why hadn't her mother said anything about what her father had written, especially when most of it was about Sinjuko? Maybe because her mother hadn't bothered, or had time, to read it. Or because she was afraid it might start a terrible fight. She must have had some good reason, whatever it was. Anyway, Catherine resolved, *she* wouldn't bring it up. That would only make things worse for her father.

X

John Sheckley, who collected old heaps and liked to fiddle with them, had also left a car at Gardner Prescott's disposal. It was a Jaguar XK 140, made in Coventry, England—an ancient black two-seater with a sharklike snout, a tattered interior, and a general air of impoverished elegance. ("It gives you the sensation," John had written, "of rich fug-you-ness that is linked with the feel of a thoroughbred.")

At five o'clock on Saturday afternoon Gardner wheeled the exhausted thoroughbred down the Welles's long black-top driveway, flanked by towering redwoods interspersed with dense clumps of bamboo. He parked on the turnaround, facing a two-stall carport, and strolled back to the entrance gate set within a high board fence. Unlatching it and stepping inside he found himself in a large courtyard lush with dichondra, Burmese honeysuckle, giant ferns, bird of paradise, and, at the far end, a moss-rimmed pool splashed by a small waterfall. A sense of physical isolation swept over him. Scott Welles, he thought, prized his privacy.

Tina greeted him at the green double doors. She wore a clingy flame-colored dress that flaunted her breasts and showed off her slim legs. Smiling, she took both his hands and placed her cheek next to his, saying softly, "Hello, lovely man." He looked past her from the small entrance hall into a huge white-carpeted living room and saw that no one was there.

"Scott will be right down," she said, leading him inside. "We have some other guests coming. We're all going to the dance at the club."

"Dance? Oh no, Tina, I'm no dancer."

"Fine thing to say. After all I taught you."

"No offense, but I *still* dance that way. You know, cheek to cheek."

"With this crowd you'll be right in style. You'll have the women swooning."

He walked about the room, admiring it aloud. The color scheme was a mixture of beige, burnt orange, and dark green, one end of the room dominated by a long curved sofa. There was a double-faced fireplace shared with a large dining alcove, a floor-to-ceiling built-in book-case, and a wall of glass with sliding doors opening to the deck. The paneled walls were hung with oil paintings, all somewhat abstract and with an Oriental flavor. A green-tiled corridor, from which a staircase ascended, appeared to run the length of the house.

Comical voices squawked from a television set located somewhere behind a closed swinging door off to the right, which he assumed opened on a family room and the kitchen. Tina said, "Catherine's in there watching TV and having her dinner. She'll be out soon. Meanwhile—" She waved a hand toward a massive carved coffee table in front of the sofa. On it sat a silver tray loaded with liquor, ice, and mixes.

Scott Welles came down as they were sipping their first martini. For some reason, perhaps because Tina was fairly tall, Gardner had expected a large man, probably running to fat. Instead, he was of medium height and slender. But there any resemblance to an aesthete stopped. As he came forward, hand extended, smiling only slightly but with easy friendliness, Scott Welles projected an image of confident strength.

"Of course I know you," he said in a quiet, pleasant voice. "Not just because of Tina. More because of your book."

"Not the best introduction in the world, I'm afraid."

"Sorry, I disagree. We have it on the shelf—well read. It deserves to be."

Liking the man, Gardner felt a spasm of conscience. A flush crept to his face as he murmured his thanks.

He sat between them, Scott lounging with legs crossed on the far end of the sofa, one elbow on the back, jaw resting on the heel of his hand as he gave Gardner his attention. He wore gray slacks, dark cashmere sport coat with brass buttons, pale yellow shirt and dark yellow tie meticulously knotted. His wavy hair, worn slightly long but expertly shaped and parted on the side, was light brown, almost blond, a pleasing contrast to his bronzed, taut skin. His eyes were even bluer than Tina's, nose short and straight, mouth full-lipped and mobile. He looked like a man in his mid-thirties.

As Tina poured the drinks, he said, "It just struck me. You must have had to take a cab. I should have picked you up."

"Thanks, but the friend who loaned me the boat also left me a car. I *think* what I came up in is a car." He described it.

Scott laughed and said, "Tell me about the boat. Is it comfortable?"

Gardner gave him a quick verbal tour, the strain he had felt easing under Scott's interested gaze. He was obviously intrigued that John Sheckley had so picturesquely broken the drab pattern of everyday living.

"Your friend sounds like quite a guy. Where did you run into him?"

"In Korea, during the so-called police action. He's a New Zealander."

"What year were you there?"

"Nineteen fifty-three. The North Koreans and the Americans were exchanging insults at Panmunjom."

"That was six years after Scott left Japan," Tina said.

Scott flashed her a look.

"I spent two weeks in Japan," Gardner said, "but I never got out of Tokyo. I was a big man on the Ginza."

"I guess Tokyo had changed a lot by fifty-three," Scott said.

"It was starting to look like an Oriental Bronx. With Broadway thrown in."

"Tell him what it was like when *you* were there, Scott," Tina said silkily.

Scott gave her what seemed an indulgent smile. "Glad to oblige. It wasn't much else but charred rubble. What the blockbusters didn't get, the firebombs did. Except for the main business section. There, all the big office buildings were intact. The gag was that MacArthur had spared that area so he'd have a decent place to live. Fine with me—I lived there too."

"About all I can remember of Tokyo is booze and women. Lovely, smiling, nubile women."

There was an abrupt silence.

Tina broke it, saying in a flippant tone, "You must get Scott to show you his pictures sometime." Slyly she added, "Very educational."

The subject was canceled by the appearance of their daughter Catherine. She came bursting through the swinging door wearing a short pink dress, almost a party dress, her long blonde hair bouncing on her slight shoulders. Seeing Gardner, as he rose with her father, she stopped dead still and seemed to make a conscious effort to restrain her exuberance. Succeeding, she darted a glance at Tina and approached gravely, smiling only after Scott had formally introduced her. She pushed her hand stiffly out to Gardner as if she had been carefully coached, and said she was glad to meet him. That over with, she breathed out in relief and looked to her father for her next cue.

A beautiful child, Gardner thought, with a high, pale forehead, a somewhat snub nose, and huge deep blue eyes. She could have passed without question as their natural daughter.

"Mr. Prescott is visiting from New York," Scott said. "He's living down on the bay in a boat."

Her face became radiant. "A *boat!* Oh, what fun! May I come and see it?"

"Catherine!" Tina's voice was sharp.

Catherine's smile vanished. She stared blankly at her mother, then appealed with her eyes to Scott.

Tina said quickly, with a short laugh, "It's proper to wait until you're invited, Catherine."

Gardner noticed that Scott's jaw had flexed. "Consider yourself invited." Scott's jaw unflexed. "I'd love to have all of you aboard whenever you like."

Scott said gently, "Honey, we'll take you soon. Meanwhile, a little later, I'll come up and tell you about it. It's like some fairytale boat."

"Wonderful!" Catherine's face was once more aglow. She excused herself with awkward politeness and then vanished up the stairs.

"Catherine has a wild imagination," Tina said. "She probably thinks the boat is moored on a gossamer pink cloud in a sea of stardust."

Scott's mouth smiled briefly; his face otherwise remained impassive. He raised his glass. "Here's to a wild imagination."

They heard laughing voices in the courtyard. As if welcoming the interruption, Tina spun to the door.

Of the two couples who sparked the living room with sudden gayety, the Spains stood out immediately. Phipps Spain was a tall, dark, muscular man in his mid-thirties who came on strong in a breezy, bantering way. He called his wife Charley (her name was Charlotte), which she responded to with bright alacrity, like the female half of a vaudeville team. She was a redhead, a bit rawboned and freckled, but even-featured and attractive because of the enormous vitality she radiated.

Both of them were tennis nuts, which helped to explain the rapport they shared with their companions, Tom and Dottie Crowley. Tom Crowley was the pro at the tennis club, a lithe but big-shouldered man with sandy hair and a pink face that, even in repose, seemed constantly on the verge of a smile. Dottie was a smallish woman, short hair streaked with gray, skin burned dark as a pecan, a cord of muscle in her right forearm. The Crowleys looked like a tough team to beat in mixed doubles.

Phipps Spain insisted on making the drinks, doing so with a flourish and a running line of amusing patter, cued to much of it by his wife.

"You might have guessed that Phipps is an account executive," Scott said dryly to Gardner, but without malice.

"Actually, Gardner," Phipps said good-humoredly, "I'm one of the creative stars."

"Creative?" his wife said, looking puzzled.

"Damn right, Charley. I create the business that permits Scott and his geniuses to make the ads."

That drew a general smile, and immoderate laughter from Tom Crowley. The sound of it caused his wife, sitting next to him, to look mildly pained.

Phipps, standing, gazed around the room. "Where's our fearless leader, Scott? Don't tell me he's in the kitchen testing that new wonder-spaghetti?"

"Fashionably late, that's Carter. But please, don't mention spaghetti. Not until Monday morning."

"What's this about spaghetti?" Tina asked.

Giving his voice a doomsday resonance, Phipps acted out the role of Carter Cornman addressing the department heads at the Friday meeting. He finished in cathedral tones: "And I say to each and every one of you, the day you go home from this office without having advanced the success of this product, that day you can consider *wasted!*"

"You mean people really say things like that?" Gardner said.

"Carter Cornman does. Worse."

Gardner's eyes collided with Scott's, whose mouth twisted into an abashed grimace. Gardner shrugged and threw out his hands, trying to indicate that absurdity must sometimes be endured. Scott smiled as if they were sharing a confidence.

"You're much too harsh on Carter," Tina said defensively. "Outside the office he's not that way at all."

Which seemed to be the case when he arrived a short while later with his wife, Evelyn, a thin, wan woman who seemed to fade immediately into the background. Cornman was all grins and bluff heartiness, courtly to the women, respectful to the men; probably, Gardner thought, the way he acted at the agency's annual Christmas party.

Cornman sat on the arm of Tina's chair, his hand coming to rest on her bare shoulder. Gardner noted that the faces of Charley Spain and Dottie Crowley suddenly went studiously blank.

"Tomorrow," Cornman said to Tom Crowley, "I'd like to do a little work on my backhand. Would eleven be convenient?"

"Eleven will be fine, Carter," the tennis pro said, smiling aggreeably.

"But Tom," Dottie Crowley said, "we have a doubles match with Phipps and Charley at eleven."

"That's all right. I'll work out for a while with Carter, then he can take my place as your partner."

"You and Carter?" Phipps said to Dottie. "Charley and I'll murder you. Six-love, six-love."

With a mock pout Tina said, "Poor me, no one to play with. I'll kill myself with Bloody Marys."

Dottie Crowley gave her a calculating look. "I'll drop out, Tina. I'll keep Tom company. You play with Carter."

Tina protested, but it was settled. Settled, Gardner thought, not only to the satisfaction of Tina, but also of Phipps Spain and Carter Cornman, judging by their expressions. Scott had ignored the conversation, his manner preoccupied, as though he were hearing other voices in another room.

After the buffet dinner of cold ham and turkey, Scott went upstairs to see Catherine. When he came down, Helen, the housekeeper, arrived to baby-sit.

As they prepared to leave for the club, Tina said, "I'll ride with Gardner and show him the way."

Gardner saw Dottie Crowley and Charley Spain exchange glances.

XI

"I have a feeling," Gardner said as he steered the Jag down a dark curving road, "that a couple of your guests wonder if our relationship could be more than cousinly."

Tina blew a disdainful breath. "Charley and Dottie? Forget them. Dottie Crowley thinks every woman is a mantrap. Probably because so many of them try to be when Tom's giving them tennis lessons. As for Charley, she feels inadequate because she can't have a baby. So she plays stooge to Phipps to keep him from wandering off."

"What's that got to do with us?"

"They're both insecure. So if they see a woman taking off with a man alone, they figure she's got horizontal ideas."

"Pretty damned unfair, suspecting us innocents."

Tina laughed and slipped her hand under his elbow. "You're safe, darling. Outside of maybe having us all to dinner some night, they'll never see us together. Except perhaps at the club. I arranged guest privileges for you."

"Thanks, Tina, but that's not my milieu. What about Scott?"

"Scott lives in another world. Business and Catherine, they're his whole life. So don't have any qualms there. What I do doesn't concern him."

"Does that work both ways? I gathered earlier that you were concerned about *him*—when we were talking about Japan. You seemed to have the needle out."

She removed her hand and lit a cigarette. "I guess I did. But something happened last night that threw an entirely new light on the fine, upright Mr. Scott Welles." She told him about coming upon Catherine with the pictures and her subsequent confrontation with Scott. "My paragon of a husband! While I was sitting it out in a cheap little apartment, bored to death, he was enjoying a marathon lay with a filthy little Jap!"

Her vehemence startled him. "Oh hell, Tina, aren't you blowing this up out of all proportion? The guy had to be lonely as hell. He probably felt he'd be stuck in that ruined city forever. Why expect him to act like a saint? He was aching for affection, and it was there. Everywhere. In Japan, you couldn't avoid it. When I was there, I didn't *try* to avoid it."

"You weren't married."

"Okay, but he was a kid and the flesh is weak. Why lash him now?"

"Why do you defend him?"

"Because I like him."

She dragged on her cigarette for a few moments. Then he felt her hand creep over and gently massage between his thighs. "Do you like him so much that you'd give up me?"

"As I said, the flesh is weak." He smiled wryly. "Easy, Tina, or I may crack up this clunk. You're too young to die."

Soberly she said, "That might be best for everyone."

At the club—a long, low, stone-and-wood structure that looked like a movie producer's home—Tina introduced him to about a dozen couples in as many seconds, then accepted Scott's polite invitation to dance.

Gardner found himself supporting strange, sagging women who crushed close and hummed in his ear as they skated about in the measured steps of the thirties. He danced with Tina, had a couple of drinks with her at the canopied bar on the terrace overlooking the palely illuminated courts, then surrendered her to the brawny arms of Tom Crowley. She whirled from partner to partner, ever the gay clubwoman, waving and exclaiming to her women friends, patting men's eager cheeks, performing intricate steps in front of the bandstand, laughing shrilly (drunkenly, Gardner thought) at intermission with a group that included Phipps Spain, Tom Crowley, and Carter Cornman.

Scanning the room for their wives, Gardner spotted Charley Spain standing off to the side of the group, alone, wearing a starched smile; Dottie Crowley sitting against the wall with a squat, cigar-smoking man, her eyes glimpsing Tina in a peripheral stare; Evelyn Cornman with Scott at the end of the bar, resting their backs against it as they, too, observed Tina and her entourage.

Gardner became aware of a vague annoyance; probably caused, he thought, by Tina's latter-day resemblance to the madcap prom-trotters he had known in college. But what the hell, she had borne a dead child, apparently lost a husband, except in name, who seemed, however innocently, to have alienated the affections of her adopted daughter—why wouldn't she be avid for compensation?

The thought released a groan—it was time *he* compensated for virtually ignoring the wives who had been the Welles's guests. He gulped a drink and set bravely forth, managing two dances with Charley, who was enthusiastic if not graceful, one with Dottie Crowley, who tended to lead, and another with Evelyn Cornman, who felt in his embrace like an appendaged stick and was no more communicative. By then he'd had it. When Carter Cornman somewhat grimly reclaimed his wife, Gardner slunk out to the bar.

Scott was there, peering moodily into a tall Scotch.

"Getting any material?" he said as Gardner mounted a stool next to him. "Everything you want to know about suburbia is spinning around in there."

"Afraid it's been done. O'Hara, Updike, et cetera." He ordered a brandy and soda. "Tina tells me that you once wanted to write novels."

"An adolescent dream. Before I discovered the important things of life." He smiled ironically. "Like big houses, expensive cars, exclusive clubs."

"Don't sell them short." Gardner got his drink and took a long swallow. "I could adjust to that kind of living."

"Yes, but you'd have your work."

"And you have yours."

"I suppose so. But it's pretty damned far removed from the dream." He gazed in to the teeming dance floor. Gardner's eyes followed and saw Cornman, face now flushed with pleasure, gliding by with Tina. Scott turned back to the bar.

They drank without speaking for a few minutes, the music rising to a crescendo. Scott downed his drink, gave a restless shake, and stood up. "I think I need some fresher air."

"I'm with you."

They went down the three steps to a walkway, turned left, strolled past high wire fences and up to a large grassy area surrounding a lighted Olympic-sized pool.

"Our adult nursery," Scott said. "For the wives of working husbands." He sounded more melancholy than bitter.

As they doubled back, Gardner noticed that the music had stopped, replaced by a dissonant choir of babbling voices, pierced by shrieking laughter. Scott led him away, across three courts that ended in blackness against an ivied fence. Scott started to light a cigarette. Gardner saw the flame of the lighter stop in mid-air as a woman's intense, petulant voice rose from behind the padded backstop that hid the adjoining courts.

"Of course I'm sure! I'd have to be an idiot not to know!"

A man's voice murmured a reply, the words unclear.

"I've thought of that," she said. "And I've also thought of something else. I—" The rest was drowned by the blare of the band striking up.

Scott, cigarette unlit, started back toward the terrace. Gardner followed in uneasy silence. The woman's voice had been Tina's, the man's indistinguishable. It seemed to Gardner that Tina had been confiding the story of the Japanese pictures. For what purpose? To solicit sympathy? Probably she was too smashed to know or care what she was saying. This latest confidant could have been any one of a dozen men who had been pursuing her.

"I think it's time Tina turned into a pumpkin," Scott said casually. "Join me in a nightcap, then I'll get her."

The bartender had just set down their drinks when they saw her walk past the door, alone. Scott slid off the stool and went to her. Gardner saw them exchange a few words, then Tina lurched away and jostled through the swaying dancers. Scott came back and said, "She's going to the ladies' room. She'll meet us here."

They sipped their drinks and made small talk. Ten minutes passed. Scott swung around on his stool, raised himself, and craned his neck to look past the dancers. Apprehension suddenly pinched his face. Dottie Crowley was racing toward them as if charging a net. She sprang up close to Scott and said, "Scott, you've got to get Tina to a hospital. *Now!*"

Scott's feet hit the floor. "What happened?"

"Tina passed out in the ladies' room. Not just drunk. Her purse is open and the pill bottle in it is empty. God knows how many she took!"

XII

Gardner Prescott did not see Tina again until almost two weeks after her stomach had been pumped out in the county hospital. His first few telephone calls, from a waterfront booth, were answered by Helen, the housekeeper, who assured him that Mrs. Welles was doing fine but was not receiving calls or allowing visitors. Understandable, thought Gardner—she was probably being devoured by remorse and embarrassment; he'd give it some time.

The next week, on Monday afternoon, he called Scott at the office. Mr. Welles, he was informed, would not be in but could be reached at home. Gardner called him there.

Scott's voice sounded strained. "She's in good shape physically, Gardner. She functions and answers when she's spoken to. But most of the time she just sits and stares at her hands. Depression."

"Is she seeing a doctor?"

"A medical doctor, yes. He's been here a few times and given her sedation. A psychiatrist—no. The medical man and I have tried to persuade her to see one. She won't buy the idea and I'm not pressing, not yet. She's been this way before and snapped out of it."

Gardner thought of her stillborn baby.

"But I've been advised to keep her under surveillance. I can't ask Helen to do that. So I've arranged to work at home for a while. Carter Cornman and Phipps Spain will be dropping by occasionally to keep the work coordinated."

"How is Catherine taking it?"

"All right. A bit confused, I think, by Tina's silences. Of course Catherine knows nothing about what happened."

"Is there anything I can do?"

"Why not drop Tina an affectionate note? Then try calling her again in a few days. She thinks a lot of you, Gard. I'm sure you'll be the first one she'll want to see when she's ready."

Two naked bodies in the cabin of the boat thrashed through Gardner's mind. He shook off the image but found himself mute.

Scott said, "You might be able to help her get rid of this feeling of rejection."

"Rejection?" Gardner said stupidly.

A pause. "I'm just guessing," Scott said.

A guess based on those Japanese pictures, Gardner thought as he rang off. Not only had she raged about them to him in the car, she had also drunkenly carried on about them to some unknown confidant. Obviously they had become an obsession. Probably their significance had opened up all the old wounds, appearing to Tina as a final, intolerable blow that pride demanded be decisively returned. But he was sure she had not planned to die; thus had consumed the pills in a semi-public place. Her emotions distorted by alcohol, she had chosen a dramatic but relatively safe way to punish Scott. Or perhaps she had been acting out a desperate cry for help. The woman was patently sick; which—rueful thought—at least partially explained her unbridled sexual aggression on the boat.

He wrote her a warm, friendly note, laced with humor, ending with, "Your favorite cousin is lonely. Why not ask me over to play?" (He had mild misgivings about "play" but decided to let it go.) "I'll call you soon."

He telephoned late Thursday afternoon, Scott picking it up.

"Gard, she's a changed woman. I don't know what

happened—maybe your letter—but yesterday she suddenly brightened up, started talking, and said she wanted to get back into things. See for yourself. I think she'll want to talk to you. I'm in my study. Hold it."

In a minute Tina came on, a smile in her husky voice. "Hi, playmate. Did you think I'd taken the veil?"

"Not you, Tina. I thought I was using the wrong deodorant."

"Whatever you're using, don't change. When shall we get together?"

"Any time. I could come up later for cocktails."

"No, I'd rather see you alone. Suppose I come down to the boat tomorrow. About three?"

She must be speaking from upstairs. He laughed hollowly. "Are you sure you're ready for that?"

Her laugh was short, a trifle grim. "Darling, I'm ready for *anything*."

When he hung up he opened the door of the phone booth and took a deep breath. Much as he had enjoyed Tina sexually, he now cringed from the thought. Now Scott Welles stood between them. And so did something strange and unsettling in Tina herself. Somehow, without abrading her fragile pride, he would find a way to tell her that the erotic game was over. Regret accompanied the resolution.

He abandoned the idea of giving the noble speech he had rehearsed a few minutes after she appeared on the boat the following afternoon. She came briskly aboard dressed in a short blue shift the color of her eyes, which now had a peculiar brilliance; the word zealous dropped into his mind as an apt description. She carried a manila envelope, placing it on the table between them as she sat on a rattan chair and declared that she was not at all averse to a drink.

"You look wonderful," he said, overlooking her somewhat drawn cheeks.

"Keep lying to me. I need it. But don't tell me I *feel* wonderful. That lie I couldn't stand."

He looked at her in surprise as he fetched her a drink and sat down.

Cautiously he said, "I thought . . . when I talked to you on the phone, I thought everything was all straightened out."

She half drained the vodka. "Oh, it's straightened out all right. In spades it's straightened out. And I think I have exactly the right spades—a royal flush, I'd say."

"Riddles I don't get." He had the sudden impression he was talking to a woman at the hyphen between manic and depressive. Which way would she go?

"I'll unravel it. First another drink. God, for almost two weeks I've been dry as a Mormon." She eyed him as he splashed vodka into her glass. "More," she said. He obeyed.

The glass clinked against her white teeth as she took the jolt. Then she closed her eyes and threw back her head, her long tawny hair floating down like a drowning woman's. Barely moving her lips she said, "The night of the dance I told you about the Japanese pictures."

"You're not still on that kick." His voice hardened. "I think I made it clear you were being damned ridiculous."

Her head jerked forward, her blue gaze incandescent. "Then I'm sure you'll think I'm a lot more ridiculous when I tell you that this Sinjuko—this Japanese whore—is *here*."

"What!"

She started a triumphant smile but it curled into a

sneer. "My beloved husband smuggled her in from Tokyo."

"You've seen her?"

"No," she said, voice quivering, "I haven't *seen* her. But she's here—in this town, or this county, or in San Francisco. I know it."

"You haven't seen her and you don't know where she lives. You can't mean that Scott told you about her."

"No. In fact, he's practically been a genius the way he's concealed everything." The sardonic smile she attempted frayed at the edges.

"Then you heard it from someone. Gossip."

Tina lit a cigarette and made an effort to speak calmly. "I've heard it from no one. And I've talked about it to no one, until now."

Except perhaps the man on the tennis court, Gardner thought. She probably had no memory of that. "Is that why you—"

"Tried to destroy myself?" Her eyes blurred with pain. "No. I didn't know about it then. Only about the pictures." She tapped the manilla envelope on the table with her cigarette hand, dropping ashes. "And about this. In here is a manuscript Scott wrote while he was in Tokyo—something he called 'Notes for a Novel.' Actually it's a complete story about a passionate love affair between an American soldier and a Japanese girl." Her voice rose. "Oh, it's so *poignant*, so *touching*, so graphically *erotic*. No names, of course— Scott probably thought that would be disguise enough if I ever came across it. But the main characters are obviously Scott and this . . . this Sinjuko. Accent, of course, on the first syllable."

As a writer, Gardner winced at the thought of all that material for a novel—one that Scott Welles might still one day write—being stolen. "After learning about the pictures, won't he be wondering what happened to the manuscript?"

"Maybe. But he put it in the footlocker so many years ago. I doubt if he's ever looked there since. We moved I don't know how many times before buying the house we live in now, just over a year ago. The stuff could have been lost in transit. And, as you know, after he got home he became completely absorbed in making it in the advertising business. He gave up all interest in writing the great American—or is it Japanese?—novel. But he's never given up his dreams about his darling little bedmate."

"He could have based the story on somebody else's experience."

"You won't think so when you read it."

"Tina, I'm not reading anything."

She stubbed out her cigarette. "I think you'll want to when I've finished."

"I gather there's a sequel," Gardner said dryly, not believing it.

The smile she had been working on suddenly succeeded, stretching her lips in glistening savagery. "Two sequels. First there was the letter. It was from a G.I. friend Scott had worked with in Tokyo—a nisei named Takimoto. This Takimoto, after being discharged, returned to Tokyo in some civilian job with the American armed forces, and he's still there. Apparently he and Scott have been carrying on a correspondence for a number of years. Takimoto sent his letters to Scott's office, marked 'Personal and Confidential.' A nice, safe arrangement—until the other day, Tuesday. It was about six o'clock and Scott was in his study with Carter and Phipps discussing some campaign ideas. Scott's secretary stopped by the house with his accumulated mail. Helen had just left and I answered the door. Among the pile of letters was one from the honorable Mr. Takimoto."

"You read it?" Gardner said, knowing the answer.

"Any wife would have. I *had* to. I'd seen the pictures, read the manuscript. I was going up the wall with suspicion, with worry. And there was this letter postmarked Tokyo and marked 'Personal and Confidential.' I was sure that what was inside would either prove or disprove what was in my mind. Don't you see?"

"Yes, I see. I don't say I blame you."

She thanked him with a lift of her glass. "In the bathroom I steamed open the envelope and read the letter. Later, when Carter and Phipps had gone and Scott was upstairs talking to Catherine, I made a photocopy on the machine Scott keeps in his downstairs study. Then I resealed the original in the envelope, mixed it in with the dozen or so others, and left the pile on his desk. When he came down I told him about his secretary stopping by with the mail. He can't possibly suspect what I'd done."

Gardner's head was beginning to buzz. He stopped drinking and put down his glass. "You've got me on the edge of my chair. Let's kill the suspense. What *did* the letter say?"

She took a sighing breath and tilted back in the rattan chair, seeming to protract deliberately the moment of revelation. Finally she stood up and said, "I just happen to have the photocopy here in my pocket."

She handed him the paper and watched intently as he read:

Dear Scott:

Well, Scotto-san, this'll be shorter than usual—I want to get it into the next mail.

Everything's set. I got your money order, cashed it—Jesus, you must be Daddy Warbucks—and went out to see Sinjuko. I showed her the dough and those big black eyes of hers popped out like pingpong balls. She hadn't seen that much negotiable stuff since before Pearl Harbor, if then. When I told her what you wanted her to do, she broke down and bawled a bucketful—every drop pure happiness. Then she started to put up some resistance. Said Amereeka wife not like Japanese and would not understand. I said you'd fixed up everything so she'd never know. Finally Sinjuko bought the idea, but it really wasn't a tough sale—she still thinks you're a bigger god then Hirohito.

I pulled some strings (yeah, I haven't changed!) and was able to wangle all the damnfool papers that'll get her out of the country. She'll leave in the next couple of days. I don't know on what plane yet but will wire you when she's on her way. As usual, I'll send it to your office.

I've been delivering all the stuff to her—even the money, ha ha—you asked me to in your letters.

So now you can start feeling happier. I'll take care of everything and see her off.

Keep your pecker up.

                        Sayonara for now,
                        Tak

XIII

Gardner read part of the letter again and handed it back. He felt like a peeping tom.

Tina gave him a challenging look. "That letter arrived in Scott's office last Monday morning—it was clock-stamped. He didn't see it until Tuesday evening. Wednesday morning he called his secretary first thing. The telegram apparently had arrived because he immediately drove into the office—just to check a few things, he told me. He was home in less then two hours. Yesterday he drove in again and was gone all morning. I called his office and was told he was at a client meeting. Obviously he was picking up Sinjuko at the airport. So now he has the mistress he's wanted all these years."

Gardner shook his head. It seemed too much to swallow. "Maybe Scott just felt sorry for her. Maybe she was destitute and he helped her out with things, then finally gave up and paid her way to come here and live with relatives."

"You don't really believe that, Gard."

He thought a minute. "No," he said reluctantly, "I guess I don't."

"But just in case you have any doubts, listen to this. When he came home yesterday, just after noon, I told him I was going to the club. I acted very bright and cheery, as though I was my old self again and hadn't a worry in the world. In a way, that was true. At least I finally knew the situation and had begun to think that it could be used to my advantage. I left the house, but not to go to the club, just to drive around and think. When I got home I let myself in quietly and was about to go upstairs when I heard Scott's voice in the study down the hall. He was talking on the phone. I went to the door—it was closed—and listened. I heard him say that he had to get back to work. Then he said, like some simpering teen-ager, 'Everything will be better soon. I'll talk to you later, my lovely geisha.'" Tina made a spitting sound. "Doesn't that tear it! His lovely geisha! His lovely *slut!*"

Gardner looked away, embarrassed. After a silence, he said, "Have you thought of putting your cards on the table, telling Scott what you know?"

Tina flourished her cigarette like a knife. "It's too late for that. It's not as though they're rekindling an old love affair. This one never stopped, except physically. They kept it up through letters, using Takimoto as the middleman. So when they met yesterday, it was not as strangers. They'd shared each other's thoughts, in a way matured together. The bond was never really broken—in fact, absence may have made it stronger. I know now why it was impossible for Scott to adjust to me when he got back from Japan. I thought it was because of the catch-as-catch-can life we'd led before he was sent overseas and, on top if it, the long separation. I thought—perhaps even Scott thought—that a baby would get us together. But the baby didn't live. Then we put our hope in Catherine. But there really was no hope for us at all. Because all the time there was Sinjuko—she and Scott had never actually parted."

She laughed mirthlessly. "I called her a slut. I guess that's too strong a word for someone who's been so constant. She's simply the classic other woman, Oriental version."

Gardner's lingering guilt at the cuckolding of Scott evaporated. Now the episode was no more censurable than it would be if Scott had abandoned his wife outright and run off to Tokyo to live with his Japanese mistress. Scott Welles sounded like a willful, self-indulgent child. Maintaining occasional indirect contact with Sinjuko to make her life more bearable was understandable, even admirable. But to uproot her from everything she had ever known, fly her to the United States, a country in ferment over its ethnic minorities, and stow her away in some lonely place—even worse, to risk the humiliation and loss of his wife and daughter—all this to indulge an erotic fantasy, to pursue an illusory dream of youth, seemed inhumanly selfish and blindly stupid.

And expensive. He asked Tina how Scott could siphon off the necessary money without her knowing it.

"That would be easy. Scott handles the finances. All I really know about is the amount of his salary check. I get an allowance from that, a generous allowance. But I'd never know if he withheld money, or if he sold stock, or retained part of the annual bonus. It could be thousands and I wouldn't be aware of it."

For a while they sipped the remnants of their drinks without speaking. Finally Gardner asked the inevitable question: What was she going to do about it?

Instantly she said, "I'm going to divorce him."

"You seem to have enough evidence."

"No. No, I don't. I can't prove a thing. I don't know where Scott's keeping her. And as you suggested, Scott could pretend he was simply helping her out, that she was desperately poor and he had flown her here to live with relatives, then lost track of her. He could have any number of explanations—he's very clever—and any one of them would probably sound plausible. As for that phone conversation I overheard, who'd believe me?"

"You're talking about if it went to court. But if you confronted him with what you know, wouldn't he agree to a divorce to avoid a lot of messy litigation? Besides, then he could spend all the time he wanted to with his Japanese girl friend."

Her jaw clenched. She shook her head. "It would be no good. He'd try to get away with a ridiculously low settlement. But there's something a lot more important than money."

Gardner raised his eyebrows.

"Catherine. He'd demand to keep her. She's always been more than partial to him. If the choice were put to Catherine, she'd surely choose to live with him. I doubt that any judge or jury would overrule her. Especially since I'm not her natural mother."

Not to mention your emotional instability, Gardner thought. He said, "I can see where your love for Catherine would make you insist on her living with you."

Tina's eyes flared. She broke the cigarette jamming it into the ashtray. "Love? What's *love* got to do with it! I just couldn't live with the thought of her being anywhere near that Japanese bitch!"

Even as Gardner inwardly recoiled from her fury, he sympathized with her attitude, incited though it obviously was more by mortification than love.

She knuckled her hands in her lap. Her lips munched as she sucked saliva into her dry mouth. Slowly she regained her composure. "No, Gard, there's only one way I can get a just divorce. I've got to see that Scott is caught red-handed. I've got to have proof so concrete that even he can't excuse it or twist it, and that no lawyer, no judge, no jury can deny."

"You mean hire a private investigator. Well, why not?"

"No—not yet anyway. I don't know of any I could trust, and just the idea of it gives me the creeps. And where would I get the money? An investigator doesn't come cheap."

"I wish I could lend it to you. I'm broke, as usual."

"Forget that. Besides, Scott might find out he's being followed and devise some shrewd plan to make *me* look like the guilty party." She gave him a calculating look from under her long lashes. "First I'd like to try keeping it in the family."

"So you're going to play detective?"

She got up, crossed to him, and sat down on the floor, hugging her knees and gazing up at him with the soft, appealing eyes of a little girl. He felt it coming.

It did.

"Gard, I'm hoping *you* might find out something."

He pretended shock. "Me? Christ, Tina, I couldn't tail a blind man in an open field."

"Please."

"Nothing doing. If Scott discovered I was investigating him, he'd be sure to think my motive was more than cousinly. He'd start thinking I was in love with his wife."

She rubbed her cheek against his thigh. "Are you?"

"I plead the Fifth Amendment."

She stood up and fingered one of the big white buttons running down the side of her blue shift. "Shall we find out?"

He made a feeble negative gesture but did not answer.

She kicked off her shoes. She undid the rest of the buttons. She parted the dress, revealing bra-less breasts. She shook her shoulders and the dress drifted to the floor. She pirouetted slowly to permit admiration of her lavender-laced buttocks.

He watched, glass in hand, not moving a muscle.

She stepped in front of him, gazing down. She dropped to her knees. She reached for the clasp to his zipper. His free hand jerked out in a restraining motion. It came to rest on top of her tawny hair as the zipper whispered open. He felt moist warmth encircle the burgeoning part of him. He set his glass on the floor.

"Ah, Gard. Ah, my baby."

In certain forms, he thought later, blackmail could be irresistible.

Before she left, she patted the manila envelope. "Don't forget these, darling. And call me in the morning."

She seemed serenely unaware that her body had been given in barter.

XIV

Gardner wakened Saturday morning feeling he had made a bargain with Satan. Images evoked by what Scott Welles had written years ago in Tokyo circled his mind in a wheeling montage.

Sinjuko dropping her kimono and creeping to Scott lying in the floor-bed . . . Scott trudging the dusty road with his bulging rucksacks, the native women greeting him . . . Brother whisking away his shoes . . . Sister proudly displaying a battered desk . . . Scott and Mama-san swabbing Sinjuko's stricken body with wet towels . . . the Captain swearing . . . Dr. Robinette grinning . . . Scott hiking himself into Sinjuko's high hospital bed . . . Scott and Sinjuko clattering through an emerald forest, cheeks pressed together . . . their bodies joined in a sun-splashed hollow . . . the family, in dyed-black G.I. clothing, laughing and drinking . . . Scott and Sinjuko murmuring their last sad *Sayonara*, Mama-san waving in the distance . . . Sinjuko standing alone in a starlit vegetable garden communing with her gods as Scott watched. . . .

And this was the man—compassionate, tender, generous—he had tacitly agreed to spy upon. In the light of what Scott had written, his present behavior now seemed to Gardner more quixotic than selfish. His loyalty swung to Scott Welles.

At eleven o'clock he called Tina from a telephone booth on a concrete apron next to a boat and tackle store.

"Tina, can you talk?"

"Yes, I'm alone. Scott's down on a pier someplace

with Catherine. He likes to watch while she fishes. She never catches anything."

"Tina, I've decided I'm not the private-eye type."

"You mean you're backing out?"

"I never really backed in."

She laughed lewdly. "No, it was a frontal approach, wasn't it?"

"Yes, and very enjoyable. The trouble is, I find I like your husband. Even if he's got a whole harem stashed away."

"Just one. With dark, slanting eyes. Didn't you read all about her?"

"I did."

"And you're not curious?"

"Sure, I'm curious—I'm a writer. That's why you insisted I read the manuscript. You figured that would hook me, that I'd have to follow the damned thing through because I wouldn't be able to sleep until I go all the answers. Am I right?"

She chuckled. "Yes, darling, you're right."

Her honesty disarmed him. "Tina, I'm not blaming you. I'm sympathetic as hell with what you're going through but that's all I can give you, sympathy."

"You gave me something a lot more helpful yesterday. Are you turning that off?"

"I don't know. I should. Anyway, you whip yourself down here right now and take this memoir off my hands. Otherwise it goes over the side."

"Oh, I know you wouldn't do that. But I can't come down—too dangerous. Scott said he and Catherine might stop by and see the boat. Remember how excited she was about it? Suppose we ran into each other. How would that look?"

"Okay—*when?*"

"Call me Monday when Scott's at work. But don't make a final decision until I've seen you. I want one more chance to be persuasive."

108

"Tina, you're a witch."

He walked the half-mile to town. If Scott Welles and his daughter happened to visit the boat, he didn't want to be there. The manila envelope was under a pile of papers on the desk; there was little fear that Scott would come upon it if he should decide to go aboard.

The main street of Sausalito, separated from the bay by a small park, a few public piers and marinas, and a row of shops, bars, and restaurants, was thronged with vacationing tourists, week-enders from San Francisco and local citizens down to slake their morning-after thirsts. Although it was morning, every establishment seemed to be enjoying a land-office business. Gardner jostled his way through the crowds until he had left the business section behind, and sat on a low seawall, legs dangling over a narrow, rocky beach. Below him, a few old men and a scattering of kids were casting long lines into the calm waters. Beyond them, white sails and colorful spinnakers billowed against the tiered skyline of San Francisco and a broken line of power boats zigzagged around Angel Island and Alcatraz, some chugging toward the open sea. A fresh breeze was blowing, only slightly tainted with the smell of fish.

Twice before, on uncrowded weekdays, he had sat there brooding about his novel. He tried to think about it now, only to find that the story line had collapsed under the weight of a manila envelope, and his characters had been supplanted by a black-eyed girl in a kimono. He became aware that his throat was aching for something cold and wet. Perhaps a beer or two at one of the local pubs before returning. . . .

He chose the first place he came to—The White Whale, a bar and restaurant abutting a long public pier. As a precaution, he passed the front door, walked to the corner of the building, and looked out along the pier. He sighted about a dozen fishermen using droplines and bamboo poles. Scott Welles and his daughter were not among them.

Turning back, he went inside, pausing atop three red-carpeted stairs to survey the scene. Off to the left, a long, crowded bar curved into a wall of mottled glass. Straight ahead, a vast restaurant, enclosed by a plate-glass view of San Francisco, was alive with diners and drinkers. The restaurant opened out to a large deck blooming with umbrella tables.

He went to the bar, intending to stand, but got lucky; a man in a black yachting cap was just getting up to leave. Gardner sat on the red-topped stool and ordered a draft beer. He took it down in two gulps and ordered another, to nurse. Waiting, he swung around and gazed through the open doors to the deck. It was flooded with sunshine and swarming with people, most of them talking animatedly at the umbrella tables, some standing at the railings tossing scraps to the clamoring gulls. His eyes tracked a swooping waiter balancing a tray of drinks. Gardner watched idly as the drinks were set down. Then he almost fell off the bar stool.

The young girl facing him, blonde hair spilling over her frail shoulders, was unmistakably Catherine. The light-haired straight-featured man who sat in profile was Scott Welles. The woman with her back turned, sun glinting off her black glossy hair, was . . . good God, could it be?

He swiveled back to the bar as the beer was plunked down. From where he sat there was no way of telling whether or not the woman was an Oriental; except for the hair, which actually revealed nothing. All he had seen of her clothing was a brightly colored blouse, again hardly indicative. His stomach tightened as he decided to have a closer look. He left the beer on the bar to hold his place and sauntered to the open doors.

Scott was speaking to the woman, smiling warmly; Catherine was listening raptly as the woman nodded. There was something about the nod—rapid, almost bird-like—that suggested a foreign upbringing. Gardner moved closer and leaned against the frame of the door. From the color of their drinks, he guessed that Scott and the woman were having Bloody Marys, Catherine, a Coke. They raised the Bloody Marys, clicked them, and Scott said something. From the movement of his lips, it could have been *"Kampai,"* the Japanese toast. Catherine laughed. Gardner waited for a few minutes but the woman did not turn around. He went back to the bar and sipped his beer. In a little while he looked out at the deck. The three had risen and the woman lightly touched Scott's cheek. They turned, started toward the open doors, and Gardner caught a flashing glimpse of the woman's face.

In the sea of bobbing waiters and convivial table hoppers, he was unable to see her features clearly. But he saw enough to determine that she was an Oriental, with dark, almond, flashing eyes and a poised carriage. Gardner spun to face the bar, hunching over his beer. In a few moments he heard Scott's voice, directly behind him, the words unintelligible. They had apparently paused there to let some new arrivals squeeze through. Then:

"Some day you must visit me in San Francisco, Catherine."

The words were spoken softly, precisely, their source unmistakable. It appeared that the very thing Tina was dreading—that Catherine might come under the influence of Scott Welles's mistress—was already on the way to becoming fact.

On the long, hot walk back to the boat, he wondered how Scott could have the audacity to meet his mistress in a public place in his own town, particularly when he was with Catherine. It was a while before the shrewdness of it occurred to him. In such a crowd of people, most of them out-of-towners, the chances of Scott running into anyone he knew were minimal. If he should meet a friend, Sinjuko could be passed off as simply an acquaintance who had happened by, perhaps someone he knew in business. Who would doubt it with innocent-looking Catherine, his daughter, there as a shield?

Revulsion accompanied the thought. He steeled himself against weakening in his determination to stay clear of the whole mess.

XV

He did not call Tina on Monday as she had asked. After what he had witnessed in the restaurant, he was fearful that a plea from her would completely destroy his resistance. He tried to concentrate on his novel, finding it, in the context of the events happening around him, dull and lifeless.

It was past four o'clock when he heard a sliding sound and a thump on the stern deck. Tina lowered her head through the entry, pointed a finger at him and said with mock severity, "You didn't call me. I've been waiting at home all day."

He waved a hand at the papers littered on his desk. "I've been busy on the novel. But I'm stuck. Writer's block, I guess."

She came slowly down the steps, eyeing the manila envelope on the table. She wore slim lime-colored slacks and a matching, loosely belted sweater. Her tawny hair was pulled back and looped by a ribbon.

"You know what's got you blocked?" she said. She pointed to the envelope. "That. You're just like me—you can't get it off your mind."

"Maybe you're right."

"Of course I'm right. Won't you at least see Scott, have a few drinks with him? He may slip and tell you something."

Gardner looked away. He did owe her something, if only because he had known her for a long time and they were in some way related. He blurted, "I saw Scott on Saturday."

"He came to the boat? Neither he nor Catherine mentioned it."

"Not on the boat." He stopped, as if fearful of violating a confidence.

She gave him a searching look from under lowered eyelids. "You've found out something, haven't you, Gard?" She stepped closer and touched his shoulder. Her eyes rounded in supplication. "If you have, please tell me. Please. I'm going out of my mind."

He told her about seeing Scott and Catherine with the Japanese woman.

As he spoke, a flush rose from her throat and suffused her face. When he had finished, she was sitting rigidly in a chair, staring with glittering eyes at the floor.

"I could use a drink, Gard. Straight. Forget the ice."

He poured a stiff vodka and handed it to her.

"They passed behind me," he said. "I overheard the woman tell Catherine that she lived in San Francisco."

"Why would she tell that to Catherine? Was she asking her over?"

He hesitated. "Oh, something like that. Just being polite."

Tina downed the drink in one swallow. She handed back the glass and waited for it to work.

"Another?" he said.

"No."

He sat down facing her.

"So he's dragged Catherine into it." She spoke without inflection, as if in shock.

"I wouldn't say that, Tina. I'm sure Scott introduced her as some casual acquaintance."

Her full lower lip folded over the upper. Her eyes darkened. "I don't believe that," she said grainily. "I believe he's deliberately trying to get them together. So that Catherine will feel secure and well-adjusted with his new wife!" Tina dropped her forehead on her hand. Her body shook.

He recalled Catherine's absorbed expression and her laughter when she sat at the umbrella table. But he said, "Tina, that's paranoid nonsense and you know it."

She gave a short, bitter laugh. "Do I? He could divorce me and probably win a niggardly settlement. How? By claiming I was an unfit mother."

"What evidence would he have?"

"Well, there was that fiasco in the ladies' room at the club. And I'm sure I drink too much. And I'm usually away from home most of the day. Helen, our housekeeper, would confirm that."

"I doubt that would be enough to make you the guilty party."

"Catherine would back him up."

"Hell, he wouldn't put her through *that!*"

"Wouldn't he though! And she'd be glad to cooperate. I told you, she thinks he's God. What's more, they'd take what I consider to be normal discipline and twist it so that I'd look like a monster. He'd get custody of Catherine and just about all of his bank account. I'd be out and Sinjuko would be in and the three of them would live like birds in a nest. Can't you *see* it?"

He had to admit it was a logical possibility. But it seemed so out of character with the sensitive man he had met and the compassionate youth reflected in the journal.

She came and dropped down on the floor facing him, as she had before. He tensed as her cheek nuzzled against his knee. But this time she looked up with brimming eyes. "Gard, oh Gard darling, he's got to be stopped. Now, before it's too late."

He felt a pang of sorrow for her. But he answered warily, "I wish I had the solution."

"If there was one, would you help?"

He squirmed uneasily.

"Would you, Gard?" She looked at him pleadingly.

"I might try."

She sat up. "Scott called me this afternoon. He said he'd be working late at the office tonight." She paused. "I don't have to tell you where I think he's going."

"Oh Christ, Tina."

"It shouldn't be at all difficult to follow him."

"But what if he *is* working? I'd have to hang around there for hours, for nothing."

She thought a moment. "No, just for about an hour. Get there a little before six. I'm sure he won't leave before then. If he doesn't come out by seven, drive away. Just one *hour*, Gard. Can't you give me that?"

"All right, Tina. But this is it. After tonight, if you want a detective, you'll have to hire one."

She sprang to her feet, smiling thinly, eyes suddenly dry. Crisply she gave him Scott's office address and directions for getting there. He wrote down the address, wishing he was back in New York.

"Phone me," she said, "just as soon as you know anything. I'll be home all evening."

The advertising agency where Scott worked had its own building, a modern three-story affair of redwood and plate glass on Montgomery Street, not for from the North Beach section. Gardner got there at quarter to six, parked the Jag half a block away and across the street—it was one-way—and sat staring through the windshield at the white stone steps leading up to the glass double-doors. He lit a cigarette, anticipating a long and probably futile wait. He was wrong.

Within five minutes Scott pushed through the doors, strolled down the steps and headed for the reserved parking area next to the building. Under his arm he carried a small package that looked gift-wrapped. Gardner watched as he got into the car, a dark blue Buick sedan, whipped it around, and wheeled into Montgomery Street.

Gardner let another car sandwich between them, then followed. Scott slowed at California Street to let a clanging cable car pass through, then continued to the next corner, Pine Street, and turned right. He stayed on Pine, zoomed up a towering hill (Sheckley's Jag knocked and shuddered), then hit a long, level straightaway. He crossed a broad avenue—Van Ness—and drove two more blocks, where he turned left at a street named Gough. He drove on for a few more minutes, entering an area that appeared to have been recently rebuilt. From the signs over restaurants and shop windows, Gardner guessed they were in the Japanese section. Well, he thought, at least Scott had the thoughtfulness to plant Sinjuko among her own people, if indeed that was where he was going.

Scott slowed for a red light, turned right, and about six doors down pulled to the curb in front of a group of low stone buildings. Gardner jammed on the squeaking brakes and managed to squeeze into a parking space near the corner. Scott slid out, looking straight ahead, and crossed to a pair of slatted gates made of dark polished wood, and entered.

Gardner hesitated only a few moments, noting that the sun had dipped behind the taller buildings, leaving the street in deep shadow. He got out and walked with attempted nonchalance to the gates. Peering through the slats and across a garden court, he saw Scott, off to the left, stop in front of a red-lacquered door. Scott stabbed the bell. Almost immediately a curtain parted in the window of the ground-floor apartment and a woman's face, unmistakably Oriental, peeked out. She was too far away for Gardner to make out her features, but from the tilt of her head and the rapid, pleased little nods, he was sure it was the same woman he had seen Scott with in Sausalito. The curtain dropped and in seconds the entrance door opened. A pair of hands reached out, grasped Scott's forearms, and drew him inside.

Gardner waited until he thought they were settled, then, taking a deep breath, entered the square courtyard. He edged around it until he came to the door Scott had entered. He glanced at the card in the small brass frame above the bell: S. Yamada.

So now he had the full name—Sinjuko Yamada; and the address. His job was done. Tina could take it from here. He retreated to the Jag.

On his way back to the Golden Gate Bridge he stopped in The Buena Vista, a glass-fronted noisy bar, and telephoned Tina.

"I know," she said. "It's seven o'clock—your quitting time. And Scott never left the office." She sounded as if Gardner had copped out.

"No," he said. "He did leave." He told her what he had learned and gave her Sinjuko Yamada's address.

There was a long silence. He imagined Tina struggling to compose herself. Now that it was all nailed down, documented by time and place, could she face the next step?

Her voice finally came on, huskier than usual, but affecting a farcical tone. "Excellent work, Inspector Prescott."

"Thank you, *mon capitaine*. I'm now turning in my uniform."

"You retire a hero, Inspector." Her voice crumpled at the end.

He said seriously, "What will you do now, Tina?"

"I don't know." She sounded abstracted, as though only half hearing.

"Look, you've got all the evidence you need. Why

not face Scott with it, give him a chance to settle this with you privately? He'll know now that he can't squirm out. He's sure to give you what you want, including Catherine. Either that or he has to give up this Japanese woman and . . ."

She interrupted snappishly: "I just don't *know!* I have to *think* about it!"

Desperation shrilled through her voice. Repeated in Gardner's mind was the sight of her limp body as he and Scott had rushed her from the club to the hospital. That episode had been triggered by no more than the sight of some pictures. Now her whole world had been shattered.

Hanging up, he felt a quake of apprehension.

Later that night, jammed into a smoky phone booth, Gardner dialed the Welles's number. The phone rang interminably, each ring pushing his fear toward panic. Giving up, he slammed out of the booth and paced about next to the unlit boat and tackle shop. A macabre image of Tina formed and froze solid in the core of his mind. He swung back into the booth and again dialed the number.

"Hello." It was Scott's voice, no more than a whisper.

Swallowing, Gardner affected a casual tone. "Hi, Scott. I was out for a stroll and thought I'd see how Tina is doing."

There was a long pause. Then: "Gardner, I think you'd better come up here."

"Is something wrong with Tina?"

"Oh my God, yes. Tina's dead."

"No, Scott, *no!*"

Scott choked out, "I . . . I just found her. She was murdered."

XVI

"You've got to call the police," Gardner said. He had agonized through all the relevant emotions—shock, sorrow, incredulity, compassion. There was nothing more to say. Action would be a relief.

"I know," Scott said. He was slumped exhaustedly on the sofa, head back, eyes closed. "I was going to do it when you called."

"I tried you a short time before that. There was no answer."

"I was . . ." His voice faltered. He set his jaw. "I didn't hear it. It must have been when I was upstairs with Catherine." He started to get up, but fell back.

"I'll make the call," Gardner said.

"No, you've done enough." Scott gave himself a shake. "Besides, why get involved more than you have to? Go back to the boat. They'll send for you, I'm sure—you're Tina's cousin. There's no reason to mention you were here."

"I guess you're right. They know I don't have a phone and would wonder why I called. It would just confuse things."

Gardner went to the front door. He stopped and looked down the long hall toward the study, his mind mirroring the bloodied dead body crumpled on the floor.

Scott stood with his hand on the phone. "A prowler," he said dully. "It's the only answer that makes sense."

Less than an hour later Gardner was fetched from the boat by a Goliath of a deputy named Sylvester. When they arrived at the county jail in San Rafael

Civic Center—a low, sprawling, salmon-colored building with a chalk-blue roof, brightly illuminated against the dark hills—Scott Welles was on his way to the interrogation room. Towering beside him in the corridor was Sheriff John Rosecreek, an elderly man with the rangy, high-pocketed build of Gary Cooper.

"Go ahead," the sheriff said to Scott. "Talk to him. But make it fast." His voice sounded coated with phlegm. He faced them, hands fisted on his hips, a stance that implied a refusal to leave them alone. Sylvester rested his bulk against the wall.

"Scott, what can I do?"

Scott, haggard and glassy-eyed, gazed at the polished floor. "Nothing for me," he said in a broken voice. "And nothing for Tina. But there's Catherine. I didn't tell her. She's asleep, I hope. Helen, the housekeeper, came over. But she can't stay on. She's got a husband." He spoke in short bursts, as if his voice was unable to sustain more than a few words at a time.

"I'll take care of Catherine," Gardner said.

"I'll be grateful if you will. You're Tina's cousin. Somehow that matters."

"I'll move in for the night. I'll phone Helen and tell her."

Scott started to sag, then braced himself. "I called my lawyer. He's on his way from San Francisco. Perhaps I won't need him. I don't see why I should."

Sheriff Rosecreek noisily cleared his throat. "Let's get on with this, Mr. Welles." He said to Gardner, "This may take some time."

"I'll be at your house if you need me, Scott."

In the interrogation room, Scott Welles was seated on a metal folding chair across the table from Sheriff Rosecreek. The deputy, Sylvester, slumped against the closed door, his thumbs hooked in his gun belt. Scott lit a cigarette, looking over the match at the sheriff's reddish, high-cheekboned face under crisp, steel-gray hair. In the elevator Scott had caught a faint whiff of whiskey. Now he vaguely recalled that the County Council had once censured the sheriff for drinking on the job. Apparently it had not been a deterrent.

In a wheezing but gentle voice Rosecreek advised him of his rights.

Scott nodded. "Go ahead."

"Mr. Welles, tell me exactly what you know about what happened tonight. Try to relax and take your time."

"I worked late at the office but managed to leave earlier than I'd expected. I got home somewhere around ten."

"Did your wife know you were working late?"

"Yes, I'd called her this afternoon. We were working on a crash project, a new campaign for a client. I'm in the advertising business."

"I see."

"When I drove in, I saw that the desk light in the study was on. The room is just above the driveway. That seemed unusual—the light—because to my knowledge my wife rarely goes in there. I went into the house and down the hall and saw that the study door was wide open. I stepped inside and—oh Jesus..."

Rosecreek poured water from a carafe into a glass. "Here, drink this. Just take your time, Mr. Welles. We're in no hurry."

Scott stubbed out his cigarette and drank some water. "I'm all right. She was sprawled on the floor. In front of the couch. Her hair was covered with blood. A bronze bookend, from my desk, was on the carpet next to her head. It was smeared with blood."

"Exactly the way we found her."

"Yes. I kneeled down and . . . felt the back of her

skull. There was an ugly gash in her scalp and a depression. I took her pulse. She was dead."

"Did you have any idea who might have killed her?"

"I thought—still think—it was a prowler. There have been a series of robberies in all the towns around here. But you know that."

"Don't I though! Did you find anything missing?"

"No. But I assumed that Tina had surprised whoever it was *before* he could steal anything. He must have become excited—maybe he was hopped up—and hit her with the bookend. When he saw that he'd killed her, he panicked and dashed out of the house."

Under the tangled hedge of his gray eyebrows Rosecreek's gaze sharpened. "Let's fix the time when you found the body. You say you got home around ten. You had to park your car, walk back and through the gate, then into the house and down the hall. Say five after ten when you went into the study. Does that sound right?"

"I guess so."

Rosecreek leaned forward on his elbows. "But you didn't call the police until ten forty-five. Forty minutes after you say you found the body. Why not?"

Off to his left, Scott heard Sylvester stir. "Well, I was stunned. And . . ."

There was a pause of ten seconds.

"And what, Mr. Welles?"

"And, well, I went upstairs to check on my daughter, Catherine, to make sure she was all right."

"Yes, only natural. I'm afraid I'll have to have a talk with your daughter. She may have heard something that will give us a clue."

Scott sipped at the glass of water. "Sheriff, you can't talk to Catherine now. It would upset her terribly."

"I understand and I'm sorry. But this is a murder. I'll be as gentle with her as I can."

Scott tugged at his chin, thinking. "Perhaps if I explain something . . . Sheriff, when I went into Catherine's room the light on her night table was on. She was sitting up in bed and hugging this big stuffed animal, a tiger, and swaying back and forth. I said, 'Catherine,' but she didn't answer. Her eyes were wide and staring straight ahead and she didn't seem to know I was there. I was alarmed. I sat down next to her and took the stuffed animal away. I put my arms around her shoulders. They were rigid."

"Catatonic, would you say?"

Scott felt his muscles tighten. "I'm not qualified to judge. Suddenly she collapsed against me and started to cry. I talked soothingly to her, thinking she'd merely had a bad dream. I remember saying, 'It was just a bad dream, Catherine, that's all, only a dream, it's all right now.' Finally she looked up and smiled and said, 'Yes, a dream,' and gave a sigh. I settled her down and she quietly went to sleep."

"I see." The sheriff studied the top of the table. "For the moment let's stick to the time. What you just said shouldn't have taken more than five minutes or so. That leaves about half an hour before you called us."

Scott dragged smoke into his lungs and let it out slowly.

"Well, back in the study, I sat down on the couch and thought about what had happened, how it might look to the police. I wondered if I might be blamed."

"But Mr. Welles, you'd been working late at the office. I assume there were witnesses to that?"

"Yes, but . . ."

"Then you have an alibi."

Scott rubbed at his numbed cheeks. "Not really. Tina—the body—was still warm, limp. There was no sign of rigidity. I guessed she had been killed only minutes before I arrived home. It could be suspected that I arrived *before* her death, that I did it."

"But didn't it occur to you that the murderer almost surely left fingerprints on the murder weapon, the bookend? It's in the lab now. We should have a report any minute. So didn't it also occur to you that as soon as it was proved that the prints were not yours, you'd be cleared?"

"Yes . . . yes, that *did* occur to me. But, unthinkingly, I picked up the bookend to examine it. My prints were there. The murderer, I thought, could have wiped his off, and only mine would be found."

"You, too, could have wiped it clean."

Scott ground out his cigarette.

"Mr. Welles, why do you think your daughter was in such a state of shock?"

"I think now that she was awakened by a commotion downstairs. I think she went down, looked in the study, and saw the body. I think that's the only logical explanation."

"That would be very helpful to you, wouldn't it, Mr. Welles?"

"In what way?"

"Because if she heard a commotion downstairs *before* you came home, you'd automatically be exonerated."

"Are you *accusing* me, Sheriff?"

"Just an observation, Mr. Welles. Tell me, did you think of asking your daughter what she might have seen?"

"Yes, and I just couldn't. I was not about to terrorize her with anything so ghastly."

"I understand. But, if you're right, her mind had already been terrorized by the actual sight of the dead body."

"I told you before—she believed it was only a dream, a nightmare."

"Yes, you apparently convinced her of that. Otherwise, how could she have gone right to sleep? Mr. Welles, how close was Catherine to her mother? I mean, did they get along well?"

"I'd say so. Catherine is an adopted child, so perhaps it wasn't entirely the same as with most mothers and daughters."

"Adopted. I see. Was there any friction between them?"

"What are you driving at, Sheriff?"

"I'm sorry, Mr. Welles, but I've got to consider everything. I've got to take into account that maybe your daughter had an argument with your wife, that she blew her stack and . . ."

"That's ridiculous!"

Rosecreek hawked. "It would explain her state of shock, even better than *your* theory. We get cases all the time of children, teen-agers usually . . ."

The phone rang. The sheriff picked it up. "Rosecreek . . . I see . . . And you say that's all? Okay. Thanks."

Scott massaged the back of his neck as the sheriff hung up.

"Mr. Welles, you said before that you picked up the bookend. To examine it, you said."

"That's right. I did it without thinking."

"But you didn't say whether or not you tried to wipe off your prints. I'm asking you now—did you?"

"It's all pretty mixed up."

"That was the lab calling. They say that fingerprints on the bookend were smudged, too smudged to tell us anything. They say it's obvious that an attempt was made to wipe them off."

"I mentioned that before. That the prowler could have . . ."

"Yes, you did. Now we don't know if those smudged prints belonged to you, or to the prowler, or to your wife—it's possible she picked up the bookend *first*, to ward off her attacker—or if they belonged to, well, to somebody else."

"Good God, how could I have been stupid enough to touch it? It was a mistake. I regret it."

Rosecreek scratched at his loins. "You have every reason to regret it, Mr. Welles. Because it so happens that our man was able to lift one clear print from the murder weapon. Just one—a thumbprint. It appears to match the one on your driver's license."

Scott stared at him blankly.

"Let's figure this out. A prowler—or someone—was in that room and wielded the murder weapon. He, or *she* . . ."

"Now, look . . ."

"All right—a *person*. This person slugs your wife and before running out makes a swipe at erasing the prints. They're blurred, so they're useless to us. Would you buy that?"

"I guess so."

"But of course the person couldn't have blurred *your* prints because, as you said, you hadn't come home yet, you hadn't picked up the bookend. Right?"

"Yes."

"But then, after you did pick it up, we got only a print of your *thumb*. But of course you would also have had to use your *fingers*, which would have left prints. Do you agree?"

Scott did not answer.

"Don't you see, Mr. Welles, that the only person who could possibly have wiped off your fingerprints would be you yourself?"

Scott looked toward the door. Sylvester had straightened. His broad, pouched face was alive with interest.

"As you said, you were pretty mixed up. Only natural. You wiped off the *finger*prints but overlooked the *thumb*print."

"All right, I must have wiped them off."

"And you destroyed the others as well."

"I tell you I wasn't thinking clearly. I thought I might be blamed."

"That *you* might be blamed, Mr. Welles? Or *someone else* living in your house?"

"That's just about enough!"

"Okay. Mr. Welles, I'd like to remind you again of your rights."

Silence.

"Would you like to wait for your lawyer?"

"Yes."

XVII

Helen was asleep in the guest room when Gardner arrived at Scott Welles's house. After checking on her and looking in on Catherine, who was also asleep, he went back downstairs. Morbid curiosity led him to the study, but the door was locked. Wandering to the kitchen, he found a bottle of bourbon and made a strong drink. He brought it to the living room and stretched out on the sofa. He drank only half the bourbon, forgetting it as he stared for a long time into darkness.

He woke blinking into a shaft of sunlight. Squinting down at his wristwatch, he saw it was eight-thirty. He'd had hours of sober sleep but felt as if he had been out on the town. Tina crashed into his mind. He groaned, rolled over, and saw Scott Welles sitting in a burnt-orange chair observing him over the rim of a coffee cup. He was dressed in gray slacks, blue sports shirt, and a white cardigan sweater. He looked bathed and shaved and his light, wavy hair appeared newly combed. Gardner sat up.

"As long as you didn't have the nerve to crawl in with Helen," Scott said with gruff humor, "I guess it had to be the sofa. She left an hour ago." He glanced wryly at the glass on the floor. "You can't want that stale booze. Coffee?"

"Please. Black."

By the time Scott came back Gardner had shaken his head clear. He sipped the scalding coffee and looked questioningly at Scott, who seemed to be under tight control.

"My lawyer had me out two hours after you left.

There'll be a hearing but he's sure they have no case." He picked up a folded newspaper from the floor and handed it to Gardner. "Here's the story in this morning's *Chron*. It will give you the gist of it."

It was a short item on page three: "Sausalito Woman Slain." In addition to the known facts, the story also mentioned the numerous recent robberies in the area and the speculation that the murderer may have been a prowler. It stated Scott had been interrogated and released.

"There's more to it than that," he said, peering dejectedly into his coffee. "They picked up my thumbprint from the damned bookend. From Rosecreek's point of view, that's five times more incriminating than a full set of prints. I'm sure he thinks I did it—or worse yet, that I was trying to cover for Catherine. Christ, how could I have been so stupid?"

"You were in a daze. You didn't know what you were doing," Gardner offered.

"That's about what I told the sheriff." He rubbed between his eyes. "Gard, I've got to go down and take care of the arrangements for Tina. Would you mind waiting here? I hate to leave Catherine alone."

"Not at all. But I'd be glad to handle it."

"No, it will be better for me if I do something."

That "something," thought Gardner, probably included a call or a visit to Sinjuko. He felt a shudder start to go through him but it was arrested by the sympathetic memory of what Scott had written.

"Helen will be in about noon to help. And I should be back before then."

"What about Catherine? Is she all right?"

For an instant Gardner thought Scott would break. He closed his eyes wearily and touched his forehead with his knuckles. A sigh seemed to gust through his chest, cut off by a dry cough. "She seems to be. I brought breakfast up to her. She acted like her normal self. I thought a good deal about what to tell her—about Tina's not being here. I didn't want to risk reviving some awful memory."

Gardner swung his feet to the floor. "Last night you wondered if she might have seen the body. What do you think now?"

"It's the only way I can explain her condition. She must have come downstairs immediately after it happened."

Gardner was now fully alert. "Do you suppose it's possible she also saw it happen?"

"I don't know. I wish I'd asked her when she was still in shock. But all I could think of was snapping her out of it. Anyway, she has no memory of it now. It was all just a bad dream that she's forgotten."

"Eventually she may remember."

"If she does, I think she'll consider it a fantasy, based on what I told her this morning. I said that Tina had become suddenly ill, had fainted, and would be away for some time. She said she was sorry, but I'm afraid the sorrow doesn't really go very deep. It's a damned shame, but she and Tina were never close. That's the story, in case she brings it up. Later, when I think she's up to it, I'll tell her something closer to the truth."

Gardner tapped the folded newspaper. "What about this?"

"Catherine never reads newspapers." He looked up at the ceiling, to where Gardner guessed her room was. "But there's one thing I'm afraid of. That damned sheriff. I'm worried he'll come barging in here to question her. He intimated as much last night. I reminded him that she'd had a harrowing experience, that fortunately it was now all blanked out, and that any attempt to probe her memory could result in permanent psychic damage. He seemed to agree, but I don't trust him. If he should turn up while I'm gone, keep Catherine in her room and tell him she's still in shock and can't talk to anyone."

"Forget about the sheriff," Gardner said. "I'll handle him." He wondered if he could.

"That brings up another thing. I can't stay out of the office for more than a couple of days—the place is in an uproar. Helen can be here for only part of the time, and I can't depend on her to guard Catherine against outsiders, whether it's the sheriff or reporters. I wonder . . . Gard, how would you feel about moving in here for a while?"

Gardner inwardly recoiled. But he said he'd be glad to.

"You can write in the guest room if you like. There's a desk there and it'll be quiet."

"I'll move my things in after you get back."

"I'll help you. Helen will be here."

"There isn't very much."

Then it hit him: Scott's manuscript—unwrapped, it was still on the table on the boat. Scott would know that it could have been gotten only from Tina, thus exposing Gardner not only as her confidant but possible also as her spy. Discretion told him to delay any mention of it.

Scott returned an hour later. He greeted Gardner grimly, asked if he would like a drink, and when he declined, went to the kitchen and made one for himself. He brought it back, bourbon that looked strong enough to blow a safe, and sat down, contemplating it absently. Gardner asked if everything was taken care of.

"Yes, but there'll be a slight delay. Right now the coroner is conducting an autopsy."

"Autopsy? Is that necessary?"

"Routine, the sheriff says, in the case of violent death by a person or persons unknown. They want to be absolutely sure that the blow on the head was the cause of death."

"What else *could* have been?"

Scott took a long pull at the drink. Then he stared at the glass in disgust and pushed it out of reach on the end table. "There have been cases, says the sheriff, where a person has been poisoned and *then* hit on the head, to make it look like murder was committed by some stumblebum housebreaker. Once, he said, they had a case of a woman who was already dead of a heart attack—she was stretched out on the couch as though asleep—and two hours later her husband sneaked in and smashed in her head with an iron poker."

The door chimes sounded and he got up to answer. It was Helen, a bent but sturdy woman of about sixty with blue-gray hair and a prim, kindly face. He introduced her and she immediately went upstairs.

"I'm going to the boat to get my things," Gardner said. "No help needed."

"It's the least I can do."

"It'll take a while. Suppose the sheriff comes while we're gone. Who'll keep him away from Catherine?"

Scott's jaw clenched and his vacant eyes became like blue slate. "I've been thinking about that, especially a little while ago when I was talking to Rosecreek. He's got that eager, hungry look, like an Indian stalking an animal. Or like Javert. I'm thinking of getting Catherine out of here until this blows over."

"Wouldn't that look like an admission that she knows something?"

"Why should it? I'd simply be giving her a much-needed change of scene." Adamantly he added, "I won't have Catherine subjected to a police grilling!"

"If they want to grill her, they'll ask where she is. What would you tell them?"

"Not a damned thing, except that I have an obligation to protect her sanity."

As Gardner drove the Jag down to the marina, he decided to hide Scott's manuscript temporarily in one of the boat lockers. Later, when he and Scott had established more of a bond, he would return it, casually offering some artless explanation if he couldn't manage to put it back secretly.

The decision rested comfortably inside him as he boarded the boat. But the comfort lasted no longer than it took him to descend the stairs to the cabin.

Scott Welles's papers had vanished from the table. The night before Gardner had not thought to lock up the boat.

XVIII

Now he could not postpone telling Scott. It seemed clear that the boat had been searched by Sheriff Rosecreek. Why? Because he had learned of Tina's visits and therefore considered Gardner Prescott a possible suspect? Nonsense. Routine, more likely, because he was Tina's cousin and had been summoned by Scott to the county jail. Whatever the reason, Scott must be forewarned.

He waited until he had taken his things to Scott's guest room and they had finished sandwiches and beer on the deck. They were alone; Helen had taken Catherine to the park.

"Scott, God knows you've got enough on your mind, but still I've got to tell you something."

Scott sat up straighter in the red canvas chair, stuck a cigarette between his lips, and prepared to light it.

"While I was away from the boat someone searched it. Obviously someone from the sheriff's office. They found something of yours and took off with it."

Scott's eyebrows arched over the flame of the match.

"Some things you'd written when you were in the Occupation. Scenes for a novel."

Scott's breath blew out the match. "How—?" His jaw clamped shut. His smooth face, usually serene, suggested a clenched fist.

"Tina'd found the manuscript in your storage closet. She said she'd also seen some pictures, snapshots taken back then, and thought they looked, well, suggestive. Those and the manuscript gave her the notion that you were still in love with a Japanese girl you'd known in Tokyo. She insisted I take what you'd written and read it, to see whether or not I agreed. I protested, but . . ." Gardner smiled ruefully, "I guess she thought that, as a writer, I had some special wisdom."

Scott dragged deeply on his cigarette and blew out a plume of smoke. "I knew about her suspicions some time ago. She'd made them damned clear to me right after she'd found the pictures." He rubbed his eyes. "God, I wish I'd realized that this thing had become such an obsession with her."

"I'm sorry I didn't tell you before. You might have been able to do something."

"You couldn't have told me without alienating Tina. Besides, who'd ever think she'd get so disturbed about some pictures and some writing that dated back to my early twenties?"

Gardner thought of Tak's letter and of Scott's overheard phone conversation in the study ("my lovely geisha"). Curiosity pricked at him.

"Perhaps there was something else," he said.

Scott seemed to reflect for a moment. "There couldn't be anything else."

Gardner desisted. Despite their strong rapport, it was stupid to think that Scott would concede anything that might hint he was keeping a Japanese mistress. His reasons for secrecy were far too compelling: fear that her presence might inadvertently leak to Rosecreek, who would drag her into it, naming her as the motive for premeditated murder by a man already suspect because of a thumbprint. Fear, perhaps, that Gardner himself, out of loyalty to Tina, might be moved to righteous denunciation of her adulterous husband. There was no way to tell Scott that the latter fear was groundless. Not only because Gardner's own brief affair with Tina disqualified him as a moral judge, but more essentially because he was convinced that a man of Scott Welles's character and temperament was incapable of deliberate murder. His insight had been strong enough to reach that conclusion.

"I guess we both understand now why Tina was so distraught," Gardner said.

Scott looked at him and nodded. "Yes. She was emotionally sick. She'd begun to fantasize."

So be it, thought Gardner. It was enough that Scott had been warned. "I thought you'd better know what you might be up against with Rosecreek. The manuscript. It might come up."

"Forget it. Those scribblings won't prove any more to the sheriff than that I was a writer of dull prose."

"It was honest prose. The hardest kind to write. I wish you'd kept on with it."

"Frankly, so do I. But men are so damned self-defeating." His voice gathered strength. "Life gives us a one-way trip, that's all, and we throw it away on meaningless things, goaded by an insane ambition for conventional success. Some men even marry women who fit in with the concept of the job—symbolic ornaments. And they wonder why they come home at night exhausted, beaten down, facing the front door and saying to themselves, 'My God, is this all there is?' "

It was clear to Gardner that the outburst was an attempt to explain, perhaps unconsciously, the reasons that had driven him to reunite with Sinjuko.

"End of philosophy lecture," Scott said self-consciously.

The sound of wheels came from the driveway. Seconds later the chimes sounded. Scott went inside and opened the door to Sheriff Rosecreek. Gardner joined them as the sheriff entered and stood tall and straight in the middle of the living room, tapping his big fawn-colored hat against his thigh.

"I just came from the coroner," Rosecreek said quietly. "The blow on the head was the cause of death, nothing else." He paused. "Mr. Welles, it seems odd that somewhere in the talk we had you didn't mention that your wife was pregnant."

"*Pregnant!*"

"You mean you didn't *know?*" The sheriff's disbelief was plain.

"No, I didn't know. Is this some sort of trick?"

Rosecreek's long khaki figure seemed to relax. He scratched at his crotch. "No trick. The autopsy showed it clearly. Seven, maybe eight weeks, the coroner says." He patted a wave in his steel-gray hair. The ghost of a malicious smile tugged at the corner of his wide mouth. "Now why wouldn't your wife have told you something as important as that?"

Scott paced the floor, weaving a little, like someone trying to shake off dope. A minute passed before he said, "She might not have known."

"Not known? After seven or eight weeks? Wouldn't she at least have suspected and said something about it?"

"She probably lost all track of time. She was like that."

"Or"—the sheriff spread his legs, anchoring his heels in the deep-piled carpet—"maybe you two weren't speaking. Maybe you weren't getting along."

Scott halted. He fixed the sheriff with a stony stare, then slowly walked up to him until their chests were only inches apart. "You're taking advantage of your uniform, Sheriff," he said evenly. "But you're in my house and I don't have to take these insinuations."

"No, you don't," Rosecreek said easily, not flinching.

Scott said in a low, hoarse voice, "Get out of this house."

The sheriff's face remained impassive, but his copper tan heightened. "There's one more thing, Mr. Welles."

"Say it and get out."

"I want to talk to your daughter."

"You can't. I've already explained that. She's in no condition to . . ."

"I'm afraid we'll have to risk it. You yourself believe she was in that room, that she saw the body. It's essential we get her account."

"She doesn't remember."

"I've got to test that."

"You don't have the right."

The sheriff took a step backward and with careful deliberation fitted on his hat. "No, at the moment I *don't* have the right. But I can get it." He pivoted on his heel and stalked out the door.

The manila envelope sailed into Gardner's mind. Why hadn't the sheriff mentioned it?

The omission had apparently escaped Scott. He said fiercely, as if to himself, "I've got to get her away from here. *Got to*!"

He strode to the deck and gazed out on the hills, seeming oblivious of Gardner, who sat on the sofa idly turning the pages of a magazine. Ten minutes later Scott was brought back by the arrival of Helen and his daughter. He tried to exude an air of naturalness, succeeding until he put an arm around Catherine's slight shoulders. Then he pressed her to him in a sudden convulsion of protective affection. She looked up at him with wide blue eyes that appeared innocent of any knowledge of evil and smiled warmly. She turned the smile briefly on Gardner, said hello, then, arm around Scott's waist, went upstairs with him.

When he returned he sat on the other end of the sofa, silently kneading his hands. Suddenly his face hardened. He turned to face Gardner.

"You must be wondering why Tina didn't tell me she was pregnant."

Gardner shrugged and waved a hand, indicating it was none of his business.

"I can tell you why," Scott said. "Some years ago Tina gave birth to a child. It was born dead. Which, in my opinion, was a blessing." He took a breath. "It was a mongoloid."

Gardner gasped inwardly. What was it Tina had said on the boat? *Down's Syndrome*. He had neither known what it meant nor bothered to look it up.

"It had a defective heart and couldn't survive the birth. Thank God for that. It was a pitiful creature. Huge skull, slanted eyes . . ." His voice shuddered away.

For a few moments there was a quivering silence, broken only by the sound of Helen puttering about behind the closed door of the kitchen.

Gardner said, "You both must have been crushed."

"I was able to accept it. It had nothing to do with us, the doctor said. Something freakish had happened to the chromosomes. But Tina wouldn't believe it. She began to believe she had some organic flaw. She was terrified that she might become pregnant again, even though she desperately wanted a child."

Gardner thought of how she must have welcomed Catherine as an ideal solution—a daughter she could call her own, physically perfect and unjeopardized by the taint she imagined was in herself. Then the terrible disappointment when Catherine had withdrawn from her, turning to Scott. What a series of disasters—first a dead mongoloid baby, then rejection by an adopted daughter, then a husband she had reason to suspect of adultery with a Japanese woman; and, capping everything, an apparently unexpected pregnancy which for some reason she had wanted to conceal. No wonder Tina, in a haze of alcohol, had felt driven to stage a suicide attempt.

"I'm sure," Scott said, "that when Tina discovered

her condition, all the old fears rushed back. I believe she must have been considering an abortion."

"Do you suppose that's why she didn't tell you—because she was sure you'd oppose it?"

Anguish punished his face. He ran his fingers reflectively through his longish hair. "No, there was a much bigger reason. Gardner, the reason Tina didn't tell me about the baby was because she knew it couldn't be mine."

Something cold and prickly ran up Gardner's spine.

"As I said, after the result of that first pregnancy, she was afraid it might happen again. There was only one sure way, I thought, to relieve her mind." An expression of sad irony crossed his face. "I had a vasectomy. I'm not equipped to produce a child."

Gardner felt his face fall apart as he realized the significance of the statement.

"That's right," Scott said. "The instigator of the pregnancy had to be another man."

Guilt hammered away inside Gardner as he recalled the tempestuous interludes with Tina on the boat. It slowly subsided as Rosecreek's words came back to him: "Seven, maybe eight weeks, the coroner says." So he was in the clear—his first liaison with Tina had occurred about three weeks ago. He found his voice.

"I'm damned sorry, Scott." He thought for a moment, then jumped to his feet. "But, my God, this changes everything!".

"Yes, it's a possibility."

"A *possibility*? Better than that—I think it's the *answer!* A man—maybe not happily married—finds himself trapped by Tina's pregnancy. She's demanding marriage, he's demanding an abortion. He goes to the house and they have a showdown in the study. It turns into one hell of a fight. She comes at him with the bookend. He grabs it away from her and—Don't you *see* it?"

"God, yes, I see it." Scott's eyes were squeezed shut.

"Forgive me. I didn't mean to bring it all back."

"That's all right. I was thinking——it's very likely he *was* with Tina that night. The way she was dressed, as if for a party. The fact that she ordinarily would never go into the study. The—"

"There you are! He knew you were working. He figured that in Tina's own house, with Catherine upstairs, it could all be handled nice and quietly. Maybe she called *him*. Maybe *she* wanted the showdown. It doesn't matter. The point is, he told her he was walking out on her. You know Tina, Scott. She'd go out of her mind." Gardner lowered his voice. "You faced the result when you got home."

Scott stared mutely at his hands gripped in his lap.

"This wipes out the prowler theory, Scott—something I don't think Rosecreek believes anyway. But when he hears about *this*—the vasectomy—" Gardner's mouth snapped shut. He eyed Scott curiously. "Why didn't you tell the sheriff when he was here? Knowing you couldn't be the father, he'd be out right now hunting down the man who was. He'd be off your back—and Catherine's."

Scott rotated his head, as if to ease pressure on his neck. "Maybe I should have. I thought of telling Rosecreek when he was boring in on me. But I just couldn't stomach dragging Tina through a public scandal. Not for her sake alone, but for Catherine's too."

Gardner sat down. "I see," he said quietly. He drummed his fingers on his knee. "Is that the only reason you didn't tell him?"

"Not entirely."

"Nobility? Afraid you might be hanging a murder

rap on a man who may be a fornicator but not a murderer?"

"That crossed my mind."

"Let him take his chances." Gardner leaned toward Scott. "I don't like to mention it, Scott, but I've got some strong feelings about this too. I say give the police a chance to smoke him out and then let the law take its course. Scandal or no scandal. You can always run away from that. If they nail him, he'll probably get off cheap anyway. No more than a few years. A terrible accident, unpremeditated, a plea of self-defense. Manslaughter."

"You *do* feel strongly."

"Why shouldn't I?"

Scott smiled wryly. "I guess I have to go along with you. But even if I told Rosecreek the truth, it might not do a damned bit of good."

"Why not?"

"He already has me under suspicion because of the thumbprint. If he knew Tina was pregnant by another man, he'd probably think she admitted it to me and that I became enraged and clobbered her. Or worse, he might try to incriminate Catherine. He could plausibly assume that she overheard Tina and me battling about the pregnancy. He could theorize that I'd stormed out of the house and that Catherine came into the study, had a violent row with Tina, and accidentally killed her. That may sound like I'm stretching it. But to Rosecreek it would explain, more than anything else could, why Catherine was in deep shock right after the murder. Also, I'm sure he more than half believes that I wiped away the fingerprints because I thought some of them belonged to Catherine.

Gardner sighed. "Okay, for the time being don't tell Rosecreek. But meanwhile if there's anything I can do to find out who Tina's lover was, believe me I'll do it. In my book, he's on target."

At four o'clock that afternoon Sheriff Rosecreek was back. He stood in the doorway, his Indian face as steely as the back of a rusty ax. He thrust a paper into Scott's hand and made a short, obviously rehearsed speech:

"Mr. Welles, this is a court order. It requires that your daughter give us a deposition, an account of whatever it was she witnessed on the night of your wife's death. You have until noon tomorrow to respond."

When he had stomped away, Scott brooded for a time, then went up to Catherine's room. Coming down he disappeared into his study, where Gardner heard him make several phone calls.

Coming back, he said, "Gard, I've got to go out for a while—to complete the arrangements for Tina. The mortuary tells me they'll receive the body within the next hour."

He was back before five and picked at an early, and virtually silent, dinner. Soon after Helen left, he said good night, mounted the stairs, and closeted himself with Catherine.

Waking early next morning, Gardner experienced a strange, bereft feeling. The cause became clear when he found an envelope on his typewriter, opened it, and read the first sentence.

He was now the only person in the house.

XIX

Dear Gardner:

Catherine and I will have left hours before you read this. But before going into that, let me cover a few things.

Tina was cremated last night. I know it's what she'd have wanted, and it will save us all from the hypocrisy of the professional mourners.

You're welcome to stay in the house as long as you wish. But if you're returning to the boat, which I suspect you will, please lock up. The front door key is on the coffee table.

I will notify Helen not to come until further notice.

Now to explain why I've gone off with Catherine. I've already told you the obvious reasons, but not the one which, for me, makes any other course impossible. I think you should have the full story—not only to clarify my own actions, but also to give you a clearer insight into Tina's behavior, so that you'll feel all the compassion for her that she deserves.

Let me go back to the time when Catherine survived an auto crash in which her parents were killed. I don't think any natural parents could have been more thankful than we were when we adopted that lovely child. Tina adored her, showered her with attention, loved to show her off. Then after a while certain things began to show up that made us apprehensive. Catherine's taste in reading didn't progress. She stuck to the same childish interests, and—this is when we really started to worry—she couldn't keep up in school. We thought she might be partially deaf, or had poor vision, but examinations proved them perfect.

Finally we found a doctor who was able to make the diagnosis. Undetected at the time of the accident, a small area of Catherine's brain had been damaged. She was retarded, her mental capacity arrested.

At first Tina tried to accept the situation, *really* tried. But preying on her mind was the memory of her only natural child—a mongoloid, born dead. She had blamed some physical deficiency in herself for that, but the experience with Catherine demanded a different explanation. So Tina blamed it on fate. She believed she was spooked. She became overwhelmed with resentment that this girl had made her twice-cursed. She needed psychiatric help but refused it, attempting instead to escape her anxieties through drinking and a hectic social life. I'm afraid I was less than useless to her. I was too busy trying to be one of the identical human ants, even though I got damned little nourishment from it.

Finally Tina insisted that Catherine be placed in an institution—schools, they call them. I opposed it. With good reasons, I thought. Catherine was capable of taking care of herself. She could comprehend, though of course not as much as others her age. She was well behaved. She was warm, loving, full of joy. She even had a remarkable talent for drawing. It seemed monstrous to me to throw her in with children who had wild tantrums, who defecated on the floor, who, in many cases, survived like vegetables.

After a number of scenes, Tina offered me a bargain. Catherine could continue to live at home, and Tina herself would take care of her, but only if I agreed to certain conditions. The conditions were: No one was to know that Catherine was retarded. She would be taken out of school and provided with what education was necessary by a tutor we could trust. Play with other girls was to be on a selective basis and would be permitted only when Tina or I were present.

I agreed. Maybe you think I was a damned fool, but it was a hell of a lot better than shutting Catherine away in one of those institutions. Besides, I felt Tina deserved some compensation for suffering the horror of that stillborn mongoloid child. And I didn't want my home broken up. That would have devastated Catherine, and Tina would have gotten her anyway, to treat however she wished.

I didn't think we'd get away with it; in fact, hoped we wouldn't. At some point, I thought, the truth would become known. When it did, I felt sure that Tina would come to her senses, face reality, and accommodate herself to Catherine's handicap. But I was wrong. Every time Tina sensed the threat of exposure, we moved. I was too preoccupied to think much about it. Without really being aware of it, I slowly began to accept the permanency of the arrangement. Tina never spent any time with Catherine, and as she had no outside friends, I automatically began to fill the gap as best I could—I made up stories for her, told and acted out jokes, played games, took her on weekend outings.

The result, I guess, was inevitable. Tina, feeling cruelly rejected, became jealous and bitter, often taking it out on Catherine. And the more severely she treated Catherine, the more protective of her I became. Overprotective, perhaps.

In the light of all this, I hope you appreciate even more than you did before why I will not permit the authorities to interrogate Catherine. Not only could it destroy her emotionally, but once she was revealed as a retardate, prejudice against anyone who is "different" would surely deepen the official suspicion that already surrounds her. So she has to be protected, no matter what the cost. I won't take the risk of having her committed to a "school." I'm sure you understand.

I've been conditioned for so long to absolute secrecy about Catherine that I now feel I've betrayed her. This is nonsense, of course, because I'm certain you won't say a word of this to anyone.

Forgive me for taking off without notice—but the decision was not made until long after you were asleep, and I wanted to make sure I got a head start on Rosecreek.

Finally, trust me, as I trust you. I'll get in touch with you when the time seems right. Meanwhile, my thanks for all your support. I'm grateful to have you as a friend.

Good Luck,
Scott

Dismayed as he was, a thought leaped instantly into Gardner's mind: Scott had taken Catherine to Sinjuko (for surely he would not abandon the woman he had only a few days before transported from Tokyo).

He went downstairs, made coffee, and sat at the dinette table, trying to figure things out.

How could he help to remove the suspicion of murder from both Scott and Catherine? Only by finding the man who was the logical alternative—the man who had impregnated Tina. Was there some way he could be identified? Gardner mentally checked off everything Tina had disclosed—the pictures, Scott's phone conversation in the study, the manuscript, Tak's letter...

Fragments of the letter spun through his mind: "got your money order . . . went to see Sinjuko . . . she broke down . . . I said you'd fixed up everything . . .

I wangled the papers that'll get her out of the country . . . will wire you when she's on her way . . . now you can start feeling happier."

Where was the photocopy now? Tina would not have thrown it away. Could Scott have found it and destroyed it, as he must surely have destroyed the original? Certainly the authorities had not discovered it or Rosecreek would have flaunted it in Scott's face.

There was another, more likely possibility—Tina's lover had it. He must have been shrewd enough to see that possession of the letter offered him protection. From Tina, because without that vital piece of evidence she would probably reject a profitless divorce and leave him in peace. From Scott, because should he somehow learn of the affair and its consequences, the letter would assure his silence.

It was a good bet that the man had either talked Tina into giving him the letter for safekeeping or had stolen it.

The thought ignited another. Tina must also have carried on about Scott's manuscript. No wonder Rosecreek had not mentioned it! It had to have been snatched from the boat by Tina's lover as part of the package of potential blackmail! The manuscript made it clear that Scott's recent generosity was not simply a noble gesture inspired by pity for an old Japanese friend—a relationship construable as platonic—but was motivated by a passionate desire to reinstate Sinjuko as his mistress.

Tina's lover was bound to see that the evidence he held had dramatically increased in value. It had now become his shield against a murder charge. For in the hands of the law, the letter and the manuscript would constitute a powerful indictment of Scott Welles as the slayer of his wife.

Who *was* the man? Was there no clue at all?

Gardner was packing his bag when he recalled the

night with Scott on the tennis court: Tina complaining about the Japanese pictures to a virtual stranger.

The pictures—or her pregnancy? A stranger—or her lover?

Three names dropped into Gardner's mind.

XX

The complete results of the autopsy were not reported in the press the next morning. Only: "The coroner certified that death resulted from the crushing of the cranium, causing a massive hemorrhage of the brain."

Perhaps Rosecreek had considerately withheld news of the pregnancy in order not to enlarge on the tragedy. More likely, Gardner thought, his reasons were strictly professional.

As he finished the item, he felt the boat roll and heard the bang of heavy boots overhead. He sprang to the deck and faced Sheriff Rosecreek.

Without any greeting Rosecreek said, "It looks like your good friend has flown the coop." He added significantly, "With his daughter."

Anticipating him, Gardner decided on an unruffled reaction. "What makes you say that?" He sat on a canvas chair.

The sheriff lounged against the railing, turning his head to spit over the side. "No one answered at his house and it's locked up tight. Welles's car is gone. I phoned his office a few minutes ago. He's not there. I spoke to his boss, Cornman, who said he isn't expected until the end of the week."

Gardner feigned an expression of relief. "Well, I'm glad of that. I urged him to get away from that house for a while. After all, he's had a terrible shock."

The sheriff's veined horse's eyes narrowed with suspicion. "Cornman said Welles refused to say where he'd be."

"Good for Scott. If he'd told Cornman, he could expect to be just another branch office."

"I think there's more to it than that. Cornman also said he wouldn't be surprised if Welles quit the company."

Was Carter Cornman deliberately making things tougher for Scott?

"Oh hell, in Scott's state of mind, who could be interested in *anything*? He'll come around. He just needs a little time."

Rosecreek straightened to an official posture. "Time is what he's fast running out of." He squinted at his watch. "In about two and one-half hours—at noon—Welles is legally required to respond to that court order. Do you know if he intends to?"

"No, I don't," Gardner said stiffly. "I'm not Mr. Welles's keeper."

Rosecreek slowly elevated his silver eyebrows. "Now I wouldn't exactly say that, Mr. Prescott. For a man whose relative has been murdered, you seem strangely anxious to protect two logical suspects—Welles and his daughter. I wonder why."

"Because I know they're innocent."

"What makes you so sure?"

Gardner ignored the question. "Are you accusing Scott Welles or his daughter? Because if you are, I think you're wide open to charges. Slander, defamation of character."

Rosecreek smiled with almost paternal indulgence. "Calm down, Mr. Prescott. *Suspects* is the word I used." He lowered himself to Gardner's level by squatting down, his muscled forearms, meringued with hair, resting on his thighs. "An *accurate* word. Welles's thumbprint was on the bookend. He'd gotten home from the office in time to commit the murder, or so it looked. As for his daughter, she had to have seen or done something mighty strange to be in the state Welles described. And now, right after being subpoenaed, and probably in the middle of the night, they both disappear. For a change of scene, you say. I say it was panic. If Welles isn't guilty of the murder himself, he thinks his daughter might be. There's no other explanation."

"He's given you an explanation. Catherine's a sensitive child. She's in a critical condition. An inquisition now about some horrible experience she managed to block out could unbalance her mentally."

"Oh come on, Mr. Prescott. She'd be interviewed by a medical man. He'd know how to handle it."

"Scott doesn't think so. I don't either."

"All right. He could have had his own doctor certify her condition to a judge and ask for a restraining order, preventing us from interrogating her right now. His lawyer would have told him that. But no, he bolted."

It was useless to continue, Gardner saw, unless he was willing to disclose Catherine's true affliction. And it was not for him to divulge a secret, so long kept, that might give her the first push toward the kind of institution Scott so abhorred.

Rosecreek said, "My hunch is he's planting her in some hideout."

Gardner mentally agreed. She was, he felt sure, in Sinjuko's San Francisco apartment. To avoid incriminating Scott, he vowed to say nothing that would so much as hint at the woman's existence.

He said, "Scott's got no one to take care of her. The housekeeper's there only part of the day. Why shouldn't he take her to someone else's home?"

"Agreed. But combined with everything else, it can also be construed as evidence of guilt."

Gardner thought a minute. "Apparently you've decided simply to forget that a prowler could have been the killer."

Rosecreek stood up. "Pretty much. When I got to the Welles's that night, every door in the house was locked the same way it must have been when Scott Welles got home earlier. There was no sign of forced entry. So how could it have been a prowler?" He pulled a cigarette from the pocket of his tan shirt and wet the end before lighting it. "Of course, *some* man could have entered before Welles himself got there. But it would have had to be someone Mrs. Welles *let* in, someone she knew." He arched an eyebrow at Gardner.

"What are you getting at?"

"Mr. Prescott, I'm going to level with you. Yesterday I called on about a dozen people who claimed to be friends or close acquaintances of Mrs. Welles. I got their names at the tennis club, where she seemed to have spent a good deal of her time. I told these people—all of 'em married women, their husbands were at work—that I was just making a routine check to see if they could think of anyone who might have reason to harm Mrs. Welles."

He shifted his weight to one foot, as if to get comfortable. "Most just looked blank and said no. But a few opened up with some pretty interesting statements. The mildest, I'd say, came from a woman who said that Mrs. Welles flirted with every man she met. The strongest came from a woman with plain murder in her eyes. She said, 'The way Tina Welles threw herself at my husband, I'd have gladly strangled her with my bare hands.' All of these teed-off women were either with their husbands on the night of the murder or knew exactly where they were. So they could afford to be honest. The others, I don't know. I don't like telling you this, Mr. Prescott, considering Mrs. Welles was part of the family. But if there's any truth to what I heard, it could be she'd been spreading herself around."

Gardner put all the outrage he could muster into his voice. "Yet thinking this, you're still hounding

Scott Welles as if he's the number one suspect, instead of a father deeply concerned with his daughter's welfare!"

"On the known facts, he and his daughter are my best bets. The other—about Mrs. Welles—was pure gossip, the howlings of jealous cats. There's no proof at all that she hopped into bed with even one of those husbands."

Gardner shifted uncomfortably in the chair. He rubbed his face.

"Would you know something about that, Mr. Prescott?"

Gardner gave a short, dry cough. "I hadn't seen Tina in years. And I've only been out here for a short while."

Rosecreek said softly in his phlegmed voice, "That isn't really answering the question, is it?"

"What do you want me to say—that I know my cousin had a lover?"

"Did she?"

Gardner squeezed his eyes shut. What Scott had told him had been in confidence. But anyone capable of thinking clearly would see that the confidence must be violated, provided there was a guarantee of discretion.

"Sheriff, I'll tell you something on one condition—that you don't breathe a word of it to the press."

"I give the press as little as possible. Maybe you noticed that there was nothing in this morning's paper about Mrs. Welles' being pregnant."

It was no guarantee but it was enough. Still, Gardner stalled. "Why didn't you report it?"

"Because of that big look of surprise when I told Welles about it. I thought that just maybe another man . . . but no, now I think it was an act."

"It was no act. Scott Welles was *not* the father."

"So he fooled you too. But with you it stuck."

Gardner plunged. "It was impossible for him to be the father because a number of years ago he had a vasectomy."

Rosecreek's eyes suddenly resembled two black-centered cue balls. "Well, for God's sake, why didn't he *tell* me? What better evidence could he have ..."

"He didn't want Tina smeared. The papers would have a field day."

"He'd rather risk his neck, and his daughter's?"

"Apparently he would."

Rosecreek scratched reflectively between his legs. "Wait a minute. That still doesn't get him off the hook. He could have found out about the pregnancy before I told him, gone off his rocker and—" He snapped his thick fingers.

"I thought about that too, Sheriff. But I've come to know Scott Welles a bit. He's just not the kind to lose control of himself."

Rosecreek scowled in thought. "You could be right. As for the vasectomy, now I can see why you're on his side. Of course, he might have invented the story for just that purpose." He held up a hand as Gardner started to reply. "Okay, let's say I buy it. That would mean there's another man in the picture with a motive. It's worth investigating."

Gardner felt the sweaty satisfaction of hard-won victory. "Perhaps I can help. Who was the woman who said she'd like to have strangled Tina?"

Rosecreek hesitated, then said, "Sorry, Mr. Prescott, we don't give out that kind of information."

"Even if it could give you a solid lead?"

The sheriff swung around and looked out at the bay.

"All right," said Gardner, "let's try it another way. I'll give you three names. Maybe you'll tell me if hers is one of them."

Rosecreek turned back with a calculated look.

Gardner said slowly, "Cornman . . . Spain . . . Crowley."

Rosecreek blinked. He fetched a small notebook from his back pocket and flipped to a page. "Why those particular names, Mr. Prescott?"

"Because I gather they're key people in Scott and Tina's social group. I met them at a dinner party at the Welles's the night—" The tip of his tongue stuck to the back of his upper teeth.

"The night of *what?*"

It didn't matter; it was on the record and Rosecreek might already have heard about it. "The night Tina took too many tranquilizers and was taken to the county hospital. They pumped out her stomach."

"She attempted suicide?"

"She didn't speak about it afterwards, so I don't really know.

"Logical, considering the pregnancy. That would seem to support the other-man theory. You say she took the pills at the dinner party, when these three other couples were there?"

"It happened much later, at the tennis club. There was a dance."

"What night was that?"

"Saturday night. A few weeks before Tina was killed."

"And you think the husband of one of these women"—he consulted his notebook—"Cornman, that's Welles's boss; Spain, he works with Welles; and Crowley, the club tennis pro—you think one of them might have been having an affair with Mrs. Welles?"

"I'm not saying that. But any one of their wives might have thought so. Especially the one who was so bluntly outspoken."

"Did Mrs. Welles give them any cause for suspicion, as far as you could see? At the dinner party? At the dance?"

"Well, at the dance all three men were making something of a fuss over Tina. But so were a lot of others; there'd been a good deal of drinking. I got the impression that the wives of Tina's guests were pretty annoyed." He thought of the unseen tableau on the tennis court but decided against mentioning it; inadvertently he might let slip about the Japanese pictures.

Rosecreek said abruptly, "The woman who said she'd like to have strangled Tina Welles was Dorothy Crowley, wife of the pro."

Remembering the small, dark, energetic woman, recalling the stare she had fixed on Tina reveling before the bandstand, Gardner was not overly surprised. "And you say her husband was home on the night of the murder?"

Rosecreek glanced again at his notebook. "According to her, yes."

"Was *she* at home that night?"

Embarrassment deepened Rosecreek's color. "I assume she was. But it should be checked out."

"What about Cornman and Spain? Did their wives have any complaint against Tina?"

"No. Both said she was a fine woman, a good friend. They could think of no enemies."

"And their husbands also were at home that night?"

"No, they were in the office working with Welles. I'll talk to them, but it looks like a waste of time."

Half apologetically Gardner said, "Well, it seemed like the right place to start. Anyway, I think there's a good chance the man is a member of the tennis club."

"That's quite a list. But there's no point in starting on it until after noon today. If we don't see or hear from Scott Welles by then, I'll concentrate on only two people."

Gardner was halfway through a late lunch when

Sheriff Rosecreek came clattering down to the cabin. He pushed his Indian face up close, stiffening Gardner with a bourboned breath.

"Not a word from him," he said hoarsely, eyes bulging. "And not a peep or a paper from his lawyer!"

Having hoped but not expected that Scott would appear, Gardner was surprised only by the sheriff's vehemence. Calmly he said, "I'm sure there's a good explanation."

"You're damned right there is! Scott Welles knows he can't stand up to investigation. Or he knows his daughter can't. They're now fugitives from justice!"

"What do you do now?"

"I've already done it. I put out an APB to have them picked up. The description of them, the car, the license should make that a cinch. Though, Christ knows, they could be in Mexico by now."

"Cornman said he'd be back by Friday." Immediately Gardner regretted the reminder.

"That's a crock and you know it." He banged his Stetson against his thigh. "I just thought I'd pass the word in case he contacts you. Maybe you can talk some sense into him, get him to turn himself in. It would go a lot easier for him." He stomped up the stairs.

Should he attempt to reach Scott, Gardner wondered—warn him that he was now a target for every police officer in the state? He considered and rejected going directly to Sinjuko's apartment. The concern that doing so would reveal his previous knowledge of Sinjuko was secondary to the certainty that Rosecreek would have him followed.

At least he would try Scott's office early Friday morning. Not that it would do any good. Despite Rosecreek's skepticism, the office was certain to be under police surveillance. And Gardner was as sure as the sheriff that Scott would not return.

XXI

Gardner telephoned Scott's office on the dot of nine Friday morning. Mr. Welles was not in, the girl said. Gardner was prepared. Could he please speak to Mr. Cornman?

The agency president came on the wire sounding bluff and hearty. "Yes, Mr. Prescott, I certainly *do* remember you." His voice abruptly became sepulchral. "My deepest condolences to you. You are, I believe, Tina's cousin? A terrible tragedy. Is there something I can do?"

"Thank you. I understood Scott was coming in today, but his secretary doesn't seem to know when he's due. I decided to go to the top."

Cornman chuckled; nervously, Gardner thought. "Well, I'm expecting him any time now."

"I'll phone him back."

"Well, yes, that will be fine. I suggest in about an hour."

An hour later Gardner again talked to Scott's uninformed secretary. And again transferred to Carter Cornman.

"Mr. Prescott, I think it advisable that you come into my office. Can you make it at eleven?"

Hanging up, Gardner was struck with apprehension. He had detected consternation in Cornman's voice.

At precisely eleven o'clock a honey-blond secretary escorted Gardner into a large paneled office, sat him in an upholstered green chair facing a huge leather-topped desk, and left him alone with the assurance that Mr. Cornman would arrive at any minute. He came striding in ten minutes later, a bemused expression on his round red face, his handshake abstractedly impersonal, as though somewhere he had misplaced his image. Behind his desk he lowered his tall frame into a high-backed, tan leather chair, rested his meaty chin on folded hands and stared for a few moments at a small silver tennis trophy used as a paperweight. Looking up, his eyes focused on Gardner's face, studying it, perhaps to reassure himself that this was the same man he had met at the Welles's. He smiled mechanically, brushed rapidly at his sparse hair, and leaned back.

"Mr. Prescott, someone who owned an advertising agency once said, 'Every night almost one hundred percent of our inventory goes down the elevator and out of the building.' *People*—that's really all we've got to sell. And I pride myself on understanding people. But now"—he threw out a hand in resignation—"Scott Welles—I have to confess, he's got me baffled."

"You mean he hasn't shown up?"

"Not exactly. I just came from seeing him. He refused to come into the office, insisting I meet him in an alley bar between Pine and Bush. I absorbed three Bloody Marys trying to get him to change his mind and come back. He just sat there, sipping soda water, giving me that small, secret smile, and shaking his handsome head. Forty-five thousand a year, plus bonus, and you'd think he was refusing a handout."

"I'm afraid I don't understand."

Carter Cornman waggled his eyebrows. "No, I guess you've been out of touch with him. Let me enlighten you. Late last Tuesday Scott Welles telephoned me and announced he was resigning. Not just quitting us, but quitting the whole advertising business—in fact, *any* business. He had to get away, he said, decide what he wanted to do with the rest of his life. Of course, I appreciated that he'd just suffered a staggering blow, so I suggested a leave of absence. No, that wouldn't do, he wanted to burn his bridges." Cornman's face elongated into a look of total incomprehension. "Can you *imagine* such a thing?"

"With Scott Welles, I *can* imagine it."

"Perhaps you know something I don't. But I've known him, worked with him shoulder to shoulder, for about fifteen years. For *that* Scott Welles, such an action is inconceivable. Why, there's no better creative man in the business—innovative, inspiring, conscientious. Oh, a bit of a rebel, perhaps, but utterly dedicated to advertising as a vital force in our dynamic system."

Cornman's voice had taken on the sonorous tones of a professional after-dinner speaker. Gardner's mind went back to that first evening in Scott's house when someone had derisively mimicked him.

". . . could only believe that this tragedy had temporarily affected his reason," Cornman was saying. "I pleaded with him to reconsider, but he was adamant. He wanted the company to issue him as quickly as possible a cashier's check for his stock and his accumulated trust fund. Finally, I agreed. I gave him that check twenty minutes ago." Bitterly he added, "In a bar in an alley. It's extremely odd."

"He probably wanted to spare the people here from having to offer sympathy—about his wife." Rather, Gardner thought, Scott wanted to spare himself the interest of the police.

"Perhaps so. In any case, he now has sufficient funds to meditate on his future for quite some time."

Gardner was curious. "It was a sizable sum, then?"

"Better than two hundred thousand dollars. That's in strict confidence, of course."

Gardner felt a sudden glow of satisfaction.

"I invited you in for two reasons," Cornman said. "One, I had to make sure you were really Gardner

Prescott, Scott's friend. And two, I had hoped you might be able to convince Scott of his foolishness. I had expected him to come into the office, you see. He had given me the impression he would. Then he telephoned soon after I talked to you and insisted that I meet him at the bar with the check and that I come alone. As I say, extremely odd."

"Why would you doubt that I was Gardner Prescott?"

"Because I thought it could possibly be a ruse. Several times in the past few days a man has called here, inquiring as to Scott's whereabouts. I took the first call, but after that pretended I was unavailable. Unfortunately, I had been somewhat indiscreet—I had implied that Scott might possibly be leaving us."

"May I ask who this man was?"

Cornman considered the question. "A Sheriff Rosecreek." He picked up a square of paper. "I see that he called again while I was out. Scott said he would contact him in the next day or so."

Like a canary would contact a cat, Gardner thought.

A little later, waiting for an elevator, Gardner turned and saw Phipps Spain emerging from a door opening on the reception lobby. Apparently his office was on a floor above.

Coming near, Spain's face lit up in recognition. "Gardner Prescott! What brings you to this disaster area? Oh sure—you came to see Scott. That means he's back. Praise be!"

"Not yet. I thought he might be, was passing by and—"

"Maybe our leader has a late flash. He just tooted for me to come down."

He turned grave to murmur his sympathy, then brightened to say, "We must have you over soon," and hurried away. Gardner watched his tall, debonair figure recede. He was the senior vice president, so naturally Cornman would tell him of Scott's defection. What would be his gut response—cheers or moans?

Carter Cornman and Phipps Spain—both had been in the office with Scott Welles on the night of Tina's murder. What time had they left?

There might be a record. Most firms required their employees to write their names and times of departure when working late—some sort of security precaution.

In the main lobby he paused by the elevator, looking at the back of the trim, long-haired receptionist who sat at a desk facing the plate-glass doors. Another girl had been there when he had entered, probably the coffee-break substitute. Did she have the sign-out book? If so, he could think of no satisfactory reason for requesting it. His eyes roamed about the large, oil-hung room. And stopped. In a small cubicle off to the side stood a lectern. On it, beneath an unlit attached lamp, was a ledgerlike book. Gardner waited until the receptionist was engaged with two visitors, then strolled casually to it.

The ledger, a pencil tethered to it, was bolted to the lectern. Raising the thick, hard cover, Gardner confirmed that it was the sign-out book. He started to flip back to the entries for the previous Monday.

"May I ask what you're looking for?"

Gardner's body congealed. The feminine voice behind him was coolly polite. Thoughts panicking in all directions, he turned slowly and faced the receptionist. She was an attractive but not pretty girl, with dark eyes behind horn-rimmed glasses.

Gardner smiled disarmingly. "You were busy," he said, managing a confident tone, "or I'd have asked." Why not act the well-intentioned bumbler? He was a friend of Scott Welles, wondered if he was back, thought the book would tell him. Weak, but perhaps adequate.

"I was looking to see if Mr. Welles—Scott Welles—"

"Oh, then you must be from the sheriff's office. Sheriff—"

"Rosecreek," he said quickly, establishing credentials.

"Yes. That's a name I should remember. I thought the sheriff got what he wanted the other day."

Gardner worked moisture into his mouth. "Just a double check."

"Help yourself." She returned his smile and turned back to her typewriter.

God, he was stupid! Naturally Rosecreek would have examined the book days ago.

More than a dozen people had signed out on Monday night. Scott Welles's name jumped out but he skipped past it, searching for Cornman and Spain.

Phipps Spain was the last name entered. Time of departure: 10:40. Tina had already been murdered.

Carter Cornman was not listed. Gardner felt a surge of triumph. Slowly it dissolved. A man of Cornman's self-conscious eminence doubtless considered himself above such petty regulations. He had probably proved to Rosecreek's satisfaction that he never bothered to sign out.

Gardner raised his glance to the name Scott Welles. Departure: 9:30. Not late enough to preclude guilt. The thought quickened Gardner's anxiety. It seemed more urgent than ever to find Scott.

Driving off in the Jag, he found himself almost automatically headed for Sinjuko's apartment. It seemed worth the risk, and he prayed that he wasn't being followed. Having to acknowledge in this fashion that he'd known about Sinjuko all along nagged at him a little, but . . . he'd worry about that later.

He parked the Jag down the street from the low

stone building and looked about for Scott's car. It was not in sight. Attempting the same nonchalance he had affected when spying for Tina, he sauntered to the slatted gates, stooped, and peered into the garden court. It was uninhabited.

He pushed through, skirted the courtyard, and warily approached the red-lacquered door to the apartment. A few feet away, he stopped. He could see the small metal frame that indicated the occupant. The frame was empty.

He moved closer and saw that the curtains had been stripped from the window. He strode to it, made blinkers of his hands, and pressed his face to the pane. The room was bare of furnishings. The premises had obviously been abandoned.

Probably the building manager would know when the apartment had been vacated. Gardner returned to the street entrance and found brass mailboxes set into the wall. T. Iteki, Mgr., Apartment 1G. It was on the opposite side of the courtyard from Sinjuko's apartment, facing it.

His first ring brought the manager to the door—a dumpling of a man, Buddha-like, with a sleepy but pleasant expression. Gardner told him that he had just called on Miss Yamada and was surprised to find that she had moved out. Had she left a forwarding address?

Mr. Iteki's eyes slid over Gardner with faint suspicion, then turned softly agreeable. "I am very sorry," he said, enunciating each word perfectly, "but I am afraid I cannot help you. I know only that Miss Yamada said she was departing. Her rent is paid for the rest of the month."

"When did she leave?"

He tapped his smooth chin with a forefinger. "Two days ago. Yes, Wednesday morning."

"Actually I was hoping to locate a friend of mine,

who's also a friend of Miss Yamada's. Do you recall seeing a man with her, a Caucasian?"

Again, a fleeting look of suspicion, followed by a shrug that freed him from caring. "Yes. He came before the movers arrived. In fact, he paid me to supervise."

"Then you must know where the furniture was delivered."

"Yes. It was delivered to the movers' warehouse—Bekin's."

"Had you seen this man—my friend—before?"

"Ah yes. He appeared to be a fine gentleman."

"On Wednesday, was there a young girl with him?"

He smiled serenely. "A beautiful child. Very blond. I assumed her to be his daughter."

"She is. Then the three of them left together?"

"That is correct. I saw them drive away."

Gardner was about to thank him and leave when he had an afterthought. "What kind of car?"

"Bright red. A Rambler, I believe."

So Scott had switched cars. Finding them would not be the cinch the sheriff had thought.

Gardner lingered over a lunch in town, then drove to Fisherman's Wharf where he mingled with the tourists crowding past the smoking crab pots on the sidewalk stands. He hiked up to Ghiradhelli Square and sat on a strip of lawn below Senor Pico's restaurant, staring at deserted Alcatraz and the sailboats slicing the bay. Nothing he saw distracted him from the thought that wherever Scott had gone with Catherine and Sinjuko, he was now financially prepared for a long stay.

And the longer he remained a fugitive, the more he would be officially damned, the more intensively would the power of the law be marshalled against him. When finally he was apprehended and the fantastic affair with Sinjuko revealed, his guilt would be so firmly presumed that Tina's pregnancy by an unknown lover would be dismissed either as an irrelevant coincidence or as a motive for murder attributable only to Scott.

There seemed but one hope for Scott—somehow, while he was still at large, Tina's lover must be exposed and his guilt established.

Sheriff Rosecreek, in his fanatic determination to pin the murder on Scott or Catherine, could be expected to provide no more than token help. Action, it was evident, must be initiated by Gardner himself.

XXII

It was close to five o'clock when he bucketed into the dirt parking area of the Sausalito marina. Rosecreek's car was parked not three yards away. And the sheriff was in it.

He got out and leaned against the front fender, arms folded across his chest. Gardner came up close enough to smell his fermented breath.

"Well, well, Mr. Prescott," he said sardonically. "Did you find Mr. Welles?"

Gardner started. Had he been followed after all? "What makes you ask that?"

"I figured that, knowing he was in town, you guessed where he was hiding out."

"No. I was just sight-seeing."

"Or that maybe you caught up with him at that bar before he left."

"I see you've talked to Carter Cornman."

"Naturally. And learned that Scott Welles quit his job. That he took his money and ran. Obviously with his daughter."

So Cornman had turned Scott in. Attempting to salvage something, Gardner said, "Sheriff, Scott has had a terrible shock. You can't expect him to be completely rational right now. I'm sure he'll be back home soon."

"That's not possible."

"What do you mean, not possible?"

He straightened up, spreading his long legs. "He won't be back because he no longer owns his home. He sold it."

Gardner felt his face collapse. "You can't mean that. There hasn't been time."

Rosecreek looked at him thoughtfully. "Okay, I guess you haven't seen Welles. So I'll tell you. I had a hunch he might pull something like this, so a little while ago I checked the brokers. Last Tuesday night Welles put his house up for sale for eighty thousand dollars, furnishings and all. He even threw in his wife's car. The market value for the house alone is over ninety thousand, but he wanted to get rid of it fast. It was sold the next morning. Welles paid the broker a bonus to rush the deal through and it cleared escrow this morning. Welles has his certified check. I also called his bank. He cleaned out his checking and savings accounts. I don't know the amount but I'm told it was substantial. I'd say that right now he's rolling in dollars."

At least three hundred thousand of them, Gardner thought, adding the cash Scott had got from the company.

"Now, Mr. Prescott, do you still think Mrs. Welles was murdered by a *lover?*"

"I still think it's more than probable."

"You're a hard man to convince."

Cautiously Gardner said, "Scott could have reasons for disappearing that you don't know about."

"Name one."

Gardner shook his head helplessly.

"Mr. Prescott, until now I could understand your being on Welles's side. You'd taken a liking to him. You'd made up your mind, I think, not to be influenced against him just because his wife happened to be your cousin. And he was in the office that night, though not late enough to make it a solid alibi. And there's the pregnancy, apparently by another man because Welles had had a vasectomy, or so he told you.

All good reasons to give him the benefits of any doubts. But now—*now*, Mr. Prescott—after Welles has defied the law, after he's quit everything—job, home, friends—and apparently run off for keeps"—he took a breath—"how in the name of good common sense can you go on defending him?"

Gardner eyed him stubbornly. "I don't think Scott Welles—or Catherine—could kill anyone."

"Writer's intuition?" He heaved a disgusted sigh.

"Call it what you like."

Rosecreek spit in the dirt. "Mr. Prescott, it's one thing to be president of the square-shooters club. It's another to bend so damned far over backwards to be fair that you can't see the truth when it jumps up right in front of you."

"Thank you for the advice," Gardner said dryly.

The sheriff wiped his mouth. "It's good advice. I stopped here because I thought that after what Cornman told you and what I just told you, you'd give up on Welles. Then if he got in touch with you—a letter, a telegram, say—you'd go to him and—"

"Don't you mean, go to *you?* You could be a hero."

"I'd like that, but I don't expect it. I'd settle for you telling him he's cooked unless he comes in voluntarily. In that case, if he did the job, it's almost a sure thing the D.A. would accept a lot lesser charge than the murder one. If his daughter did it, he can be even more optimistic. She's a minor. She could have been acting in self-defense. I think any decent judge would rule it a tragic accident. It could be settled in his chambers and she'd go free."

If only it was that simple.

The sheriff reached for the door handle. "Will you think about this, Mr. Prescott?"

"Yes, I'll think about it."

Instead his mind raced with the urgency of finding the man who had impregnated Tina.

Tomorrow was Saturday. A good day, Gardner thought, to make use of his guest privileges at the tennis club.

XXIII

Directly in front of Gardner, on the number one court, Tom Crowley, the club pro, wrapped an arm around Charley Spain. (What was her real name? Charlotte.) He gripped her wrist and guided her racquet through a shallow arc, back and forth, perhaps ten times.

"You see?" he said. "Just an easy follow-through. Relaxed. Natural. Got it?"

"She's got it," his wife Dottie said impatiently, squinting into the bright sun. She stood on the other side of the net, rapidly bouncing a ball. She produced a tight but relenting smile. "It's a good thing Phipps isn't here."

Charley turned her freckle-dusted face to smile mischievously at Crowley. He gave her angular shoulder a pat and dropped his arm. Pretending a wounded look, he winked elaborately at Gardner sitting on the top step of the low terrace. Sanctimoniously he said, "Just doing my job, dear."

Gardner grinned at him, nodding his head in mocking agreement. He wondered if the job required Crowley to be a superstud for frustrated wives.

The three on the court had paused to greet him when he had strolled out from the clubhouse shortly before. Phipps Spain and Carter Cornman were working at the office but were expected for lunch. Would Gardner join them? Glad to, he had said. They had resumed Charley's practice session without mentioning Tina.

It was not yet eleven o'clock and there were still a

couple of idle courts. The tennis buffs had just begun to gather, but most of them sat at glass-topped tables off to the sides of the terrace, fortifying themselves with screwdrivers and Bloody Marys and ramos fizzes.

Tom Crowley came and sat with Gardner, watching Charley to see if his instruction had taken. He ran a hand through his sandy hair and, without taking his eyes from the court, said, "Can't tell you how shocked, really sorry, we are about Tina. Unbelievable. Must be hell on Scott. How's he taking it?"

"It hit him pretty hard, naturally. But he's managing."

Crowley opened his mouth wide to stretch his pink face, then massaged his cheeks. "There's been nothing in the paper, except the notice that she was cremated. So we—Dottie—called him at his office. He wasn't there. Carter—you remember Carter Cornman, Scott's boss—Carter told Dottie that Scott and Catherine had gone away for a while."

"Yes."

"Best thing he could do. *Charley!* You tightened up!"

Charley Spain berated herself with a toss of her hair, then clowned a wobbly walk to the net and retrieved the ball. Laughter rippled from the drinking audience.

"Any idea when they'll be back?"

"Scott didn't say. Cornman or Spain might know. They worked with him." Gardner used the past tense deliberately.

Tom Crowley didn't pick it up.

"You might ask them at lunch," Gardner said.

Crowley was silent, observing the players. Gardner extended his gaze to the corner of the far court, where he and Scott had stood on the night they had

174

overheard Tina. Could Crowley have been her confidant?

Swinging his big shoulders around, Crowley faced Gardner with a quizzical expression. "Cremation," he said. "That seemed strange."

"Oh, I don't know. More and more people are having it done."

"Dottie wondered if there'd been an autopsy."

Dottie? Or her husband?

Gardner evaded the probe. "I guess you saw what the coroner reported. There was no question about the cause of death."

"Probably some goddamn hippie!" Crowley said, his voice heating up. "They've just about taken over this town."

"I don't think the sheriff's ready to settle for that."

"Why not?" His fingers tapped a rhythm on the strings of his racquet.

"He didn't say exactly. But when he talked to me I got the feeling he wondered whether Tina might have known whoever it was, that she willingly let him in." Hastily he added, "Before Scott got home. He was working that night, you know."

Crowley pondered that. "You could be right. The sheriff talked to Dottie—all of Tina's friends, I guess. Asked if she knew of anyone who might have had it in for Tina."

"What did she say?"

"Say? What *could* she say, except that everyone who knew Tina loved her, the same way Dottie did."

A strangling sort of love, Gardner thought.

"Christ, he even had the gall to ask Dottie if I was home that night. *Me!*" He popped his eyes incredulously, then broke into a grin. "What the hell, as a taxpayer I should be happy we've got such a gung-ho sheriff. Even though I hear he likes his schnapps." He chuckled. "Anyway, Mr. Thomas Crowley was in his downstairs shop that night working over a hot lathe."

Charley and Dottie strolled over.

"Okay, champ," Dottie said, "enough of this goofing off. How about hitting a few with Charley. I'll keep Gardner company."

Gardner sensed she wanted to pump him about Tina.

Tom Crowley may have sensed it, too. He said, "Got a better idea. Gardner, why not join us in doubles? You and Dottie against Charley and me. That way I can give Charley some pointers as we're playing. On-the-job training—the best way."

Gardner touched his blue sports shirt and light-gray slacks. "Dressed like this? I'd be thrown out."

"No problem. I've got two extra sets of whites in the locker, freshly laundered. Plus tennis shoes and socks. Should be a perfect fit."

"I should also mention I'm a lousy player."

"That will balance it out," Charley said. "So am I."

It was settled. To his own advantage, Gardner hoped—he wanted them to feel at ease with him before joining Cornman and Spain at lunch.

In the one set they played, Gardner hardly worked up a sweat, thanks to Dottie Crowley. Her taut, brown figure was all over the court—volleying in the forecourt, chasing back for lobs, racing to the sidelines to scoop up a shot—competing with all the ferocity of a finalist at Forest Hills. What little he was called on to do, Gardner managed adequately. Charley Spain played with awkward determination, often being forced out of position, but saved time and again by Tom Crowley's experienced maneuvering.

"Set point," Dottie announced at last, and it was over—she and Gardner winning seven to five.

"And match," called Phipps Spain from the terrace. He and Carter Cornman were standing together, receiving drinks from a white-jacketed attendant. Both wore business suits.

They greeted Gardner heartily, but in a bemused manner, as if wondering which of the other players had invited him.

"I didn't expect to be drafted as an athlete," Gardner said. "I was just stopping by to look around. The Welleses arranged guest privileges."

The name produced a short silence, broken by Phipps: "Be *our* guest. Let's get a table in the bar."

"We've already invited Gardner for lunch," Charley said.

"Great."

"It will be my privilege to be the host," said Cornman, his florid moon-face benign.

"Don't let him fool you," Phipps said to Gardner. "The company will pick up the tab. After all, we worked like donkeys this morning."

Cornman smiled with pompous indulgence.

Gardner said to Crowley, "Shouldn't we change?"

"Why bother. We'll be going at it again after lunch."

Not me, Gardner assured himself, but thought it wiser to conform.

"Well, this racqueteer is changing," Charley said. "Save me a good seat." She fluttered her lashes at Phipps. "That means next to you, darling."

She went off alone. Dottie, looking fresh, her gray-streaked hair unruffled, moved with the others toward the bar.

They sat around a circular table some distance from the long bar and next to a huge plate-glass window overlooking the swimming pool. Only a scattering of people were about, most of them having brunch. Cornman gestured to a waiter and they ordered drinks, Phipps specifying a gin and tonic for his wife. They made small talk, directing it at Gardner.

("And how do you like San Francisco?") Soon after the drinks were served, Charley arrived, wearing white duck pants and a shocking-pink blouse.

Tom Crowley raised his glass and said solemnly, "Here's to Scott. I wish he was here."

As they hoisted their drinks, Gardner noticed that all their faces were expressionless, except Carter Cornman's: he was frowning at the white tablecloth.

"Maybe Scott will be back next weekend," Dottie said. She gazed at her husband. "We should arrange something."

"Hell, yes," he said with enthusiasm.

They seemed, thought Gardner, almost embarrassingly aware that Crowley's tenure as pro depended heavily upon maintaining the friendship of influential members. Could Dottie's hostility toward Tina have been incited less by jealousy than by concern for her husband's job?

Cornman set down his glass as he might a gavel. "I'm afraid," he said somberly, "that Scott Welles will not be coming back."

The Crowleys' eyes showed surprise. The Spains' faces were blank; Phipps, of course, had heard the story and passed it on to Charley, or most of it.

"Scott has resigned from the firm. And this morning"—Cornman paused to glance at Gardner, then studied the short copper table lamp—"this morning I learned he has sold his house."

So he had talked again to Rosecreek.

The Crowleys' surprise became audible, Charley now joining in.

"I saw him for the last time yesterday. I don't know where he is now, or where he plans to live. But I doubt we will be seeing him again."

After a silence, Dottie said, "I don't get his quitting his job. But moving away from here after what happened—that I can understand."

"Sure," said Tom.

"Oh, the poor man," Charley said, grasping her husband's arm. Phipps responded with a sad shake of the head. Charley turned to Gardner. "Didn't he tell you where he was going? I thought he might, considering, well, your relation to Tina." Her light, sun-scorched skin suddenly flushed. "Heavens, I've been meaning to tell you how sorry I am. I know Phipps talked to you."

"And I, too," Dottie said perfunctorily.

"Thank you. No, he didn't say where he was going. I don't think he knew for sure. He was in a bit of a daze."

"Who wouldn't be," Phipps said.

"He just left me the door key and took off with Catherine. He did say he'd be in touch. I expect I'll hear from him soon."

"Odd that he'd leave you the key," Cornman said, "when he was selling the house."

Gardner took time to sip his drink. "He knew I'd turn it over to the new owners."

Phipps rattled the ice in his glass. Cornman ordered another round. Gardner had been wanting to go to the men's room and now he excused himself.

"*That's* what I forgot," Tom Crowley said jovially. "Come on, I'll lead the way."

Returning and approaching the table, they heard Charley Spain say, "And to think Tina never even should have been there. I can't forgive myself!"

Gardner saw Phipp's hand close over hers. To comfort her, or to turn her off?

There was a general preoccupation with the fresh drinks as Crowley and Gardner sat down.

"I heard you mention Tina," Gardner said to Charley. "Don't stop on my account. I don't mind talking about her."

Dottie said, "It was nothing really important. Anyone for lunch?"

"But it *was!*" Charley burst out. She bit her lower lip.

"You might as well tell him now," Phipps said, and withdrew his hand.

Charley took a gulp of her drink. "Well, that Monday night—the night the awful thing happened to Tina—a group of women—a committee—were meeting here at the club to plan the fall events. I was in charge of the tournaments and Tina headed up entertainment. Well, it was past the meeting time and Tina hadn't shown up, so I phoned her at home. She said she was just about to call us, that she wasn't feeling well, and to go ahead without her. I didn't think she was really sick, just sort of down, the way she got sometimes. So I told her we needed her badly—and we did—and also it would do her good to get out of the house. That didn't budge her—she still said no. I gave up."

"Sounds like you did all you could," Gardner said.

"No. No, I didn't." She looked mournfully at Dottie Crowley.

"Forget it," Dottie said. "It's all over the dam."

"Dottie, you wanted to call her back. You could have convinced her to come, I know it. But I talked you out of it."

Gardner's scalp tingled. So Dottie Crowley had not been at home that night!

"And here we were," Charley said, "until eleven o'clock that night. If Tina had come, she'd be alive!"

Had Tom Crowley really been working over a hot lathe all that time?

Charley's eyes had dampened. Phipps rubbed her shoulder and said with gruff tenderness, "Stop beating yourself, Charley. When you talked Dottie out of calling, you were just being considerate of Tina."

Carter Cornman said, "I suggest we order lunch."

"Just don't make it spaghetti," Phipps said, and the tension was relieved.

As soon as he had devoured a clubhouse sandwich, Tom Crowley got up "to see about some things." The others lingered over coffee. Phipps suggested to Charley that they hit a few before they took on a doubles team, and left to change his clothes. Cornman, after signing the bill, soon followed. Gardner accompanied the wives to the terrace, where they waited quietly in the shade.

When Phipps and Carter returned, Gardner thanked them all and said good-bye, finding it easy to resist their half-hearted urging to stay for a set of doubles—they already had a foursome.

Tom Crowley was not in sight as he left the terrace. Nor was he visible in the locker room. After changing, Gardner folded the borrowed tennis outfit neatly and placed it on the low bench in front of Crowley's locker.

He stopped at a few stores in town, then returned to the boat and sat on the deck, reviewing what he had learned at the club. A fragment of the luncheon conversation—something Cornman had said—suddenly rose in his mind.

He jammed a hand into his pocket and from the pile of small change extracted his ring of keys. He made a quick count. Where there had been eight keys there were now seven.

The missing key was the one to Scott Welles's house.

XXIV

He fingered the remaining keys, identifying each—key to his mother's apartment in New York, two keys (ignition and trunk) to his old left-behind Ford, two keys to the Jag, key to the boat hatch, key to the boat lockers. Seven.

He remembered attaching the eighth key while still sitting in the Jag right after leaving Scott's empty house. He held the circle of brass closer and examined the slit through which the keys had been forced. It was slightly sprung. Possibly Scott's key had dropped off. He emptied his pocket on the deck and fished through the change. No key. In the car? He was out and back in less than ten minutes, empty-handed. While searching the Jag he had mentally retraced his route in town—grocery store, stationery, newsstand; not once had he taken the ring from his pocket.

But of course the key could have disappeared any time during the past few days. He had never bothered to look.

Was someone relying on just such an oversight—that among eight keys he would scarcely notice the absence of one, particularly when he had no use for it? Or if he did notice, would think it had been lost in any of a dozen places?

He had hung his clothes in an unlocked locker. Scott's key had been mentioned at lunch. Tom Crowley had been the first to leave the table. Then Phipps Spain. Then Carter Cornman.

One of them, he was convinced, had taken the key.

Why? The answer flashed like a lightning bolt—*to plant Scott's manuscript and Tak's letter!*

Obviously Tina's lover could not simply come forward with the evidence, prime though it was. So of course—with Scott gone and the house standing empty, the timing was perfect. The evidence need merely be "returned" for others to discover.

Should he call Rosecreek? Gardner weighed the risks.

On the one hand, if the sheriff still had the slightest doubt that Scott had reason to kill his wife, the discovery of this new evidence would remove it. The manuscript and Tak's letter, while mercifully diverting attention from Catherine, would reinforce what already appeared to be an overwhelming case against Scott.

On the other hand, if Tina's lover could be caught red-handed returning the evidence, it would be abundantly clear to Rosecreek that the man was seeking to frame Scott for a murder he himself had committed.

It was worth the risk to Scott, Gardner concluded. Never would such an opportune moment occur again—it seemed almost a gift.

He called Rosecreek from the phone booth near the parking lot.

Sheriff Rosecreek was not in his office. When would he be back? Not before five. Could he somehow be reached—it was urgent. Please state your name and the phone number you're calling from. Gardner so stated. The voice would see what could be done. Immediately? Yes, immediately.

Pacing about outside the booth, tension began building inside Gardner much as it had on the night of the murder. This time, however, the tension was not rooted in fear, but in an exhilarating sense of imminent triumph.

Fifteen minutes later the screaming phone spun him around and into the booth.

"Prescott?"

"Yes, Sheriff."

"You've heard from Welles?"

"No. *Better* than that." Excitedly Gardner told him of his visit to the club, the mention of the key, the apparent theft.

"You could have lost it someplace else. And at some other time—*before* you went to the club."

"No, I'm sure it was taken from the locker."

"You had it when you arrived there? You checked it?"

"Well, no . . ."

"Mr. Prescott, you just won't give up, will you?"

"Damnit, Sheriff, it was too much of a coincidence! One of those men wants to get into that house. Tonight, probably, before he thinks I'll miss the key."

"Why? Give me one good reason."

"I don't know. Maybe to find something. Or maybe to plant something that would incriminate Scott."

Gardner heard a spitting sound. "Scott Welles has already incriminated himself."

"My God, your closed mind! All right. Maybe this will open it up. Tom Crowley—the club pro—his alibi for the night of the murder has a big hole in it."

"Mr. Prescott—"

"His wife told you he was home. But her word isn't worth a damn. She was at the club that night, at a meeting, until after eleven o'clock."

"Mr. Prescott, I *know* that. I checked it out. I also talked to Crowley's neighbors. They said they *heard* him working in his shop."

"*All* that time?"

"They didn't keep a minute-by-minute report, if that's what you want."

Gardner banged the glass wall. "Are you going to stake out that house or not?"

"Look, Mr. Prescott, we've got a lot of territory to cover. And we're understaffed. We can't go chasing off in all directions just to satisfy every little suspicion."

"*Little* suspicion!"

"Yes, little. The big suspicion—I say a sure thing—we're working on: Scott and Catherine Welles."

"Then that's your last word?"

"Unless you have something else."

"Only that you're making one hell of a mistake and you'll end up looking like a damned fool."

A crackling pause. Then, in a slow, rusty voice, "Mr. Prescott, I learned a long time ago that it's a waste of time trying to reason with a fanatic."

Gardner hung up.

Fanatic! Was there a worse fanatic than Rosecreek! Gardner cursed him uncontrollably all the way back to the boat.

Now there was no alternative. Tonight he would have to keep a solitary vigil at Scott Welles's former house.

XXV

Darkness was beginning to gather when Gardner pointed the Jag toward the hills, where a huge hump of fog was writhing in from the bay. Halfway up he ran into it, thick and wet. He turned on the windshield wipers and craned his head forward. Keeping the car in low gear, he ascended the snaking road with grinding slowness. The fog began to thin out.

Reaching the inclined street below the rear of the house, he backed over the curb into an open space, away from the overhead street light. Getting out, he pressed the door shut, the latch clicking in the silence like a shotgun being cocked. Above, through the deformed branches of the oaks, the structure loomed like some gray gothic monster haunted by swirling ectoplasmic shapes formed by the fog. He worked his way stealthily up the tree-lined street, rounding the hairpin corner and approaching the long driveway that ran in from the opposite side.

The crack of a branch jerked him to a stop, inducing a spinal chill. For a full two minutes his feet refused to budge. Then, rationalizing that the sound had been produced by some animal, a raccoon perhaps, he slithered ahead to the driveway. He paused and glanced around at the wisps of fog ghosting through the trees before moving into deeper darkness. Finally, twigs crackling underfoot, he maneuvered behind the thick trunk of a bordering redwood. Peering around from one side or the other, he could glimpse both the silhouetted front gate and the black strip of driveway. Gripping the rough bark of the redwood, he waited.

And waited. Only the occasional distant yelp of a dog indicated the existence of life. When his legs began aching, he risked lighting a match to consult his watch. Almost ten o'clock. He had been there for most of an hour. Disappointment sank to depression, marked by a groaning sense of futility. The sheriff had probably been right: the key had vanished at some place other than the tennis club. No one would come.

He endured the surveillance for another hour, alternately crouching and straightening, then gave it up. The man he had so sorely waited for was now probably half smashed at a Saturday-night party.

He was in the Jag, about to step on the starter, when a speck of light brushed the corner of his eye. Quickly he rolled down the window and stuck his head out. Something had flashed through the oaks. It had hit the darkness, dissolved in the fog, and was gone. He fastened his eyes on the house. Ten, twenty seconds passed. Then it came again, an instant, stabbing fragment of light, darting to a radius of a dozen feet and immediately extinguished. A flashlight beam. Coming from the second floor. Catherine's room. He eased down the door handle and sidled to the street.

He kept his eyes on Catherine's room, waiting for another flash. But the wall of darkness was broken only by the undulating veil of fog. He cupped his ear, straining to catch some sound. Silence. Then—a door squeaking open at the rear of the house directly above. He ducked across the street, crouched against the bank, and distended his eyes. An amorphous shape appeared to be mounted on the concrete apron outside the door. It stirred and he heard the click of the closing door. The shape lumbered toward him and he could see arms stretching out to the trunks of the oaks for support. He was about to creep back to the car when the figure veered off to his left. There was a thrashing sound as it picked up speed. Suddenly it burst from the hillside and bounded down the street in the direction Gardner had come from. He watched without recognition as it disappeared into the milky blackness.

Breath suspended, he heard a car roar to a start and gun away. No sooner had he exhaled than his senses recoiled from the savage slamming-on of brakes, the insane squeal of tires. The man had apparently overshot the turn. Gardner listened for the sound of an engine but heard nothing.

Now the engine sound. But this time close and from the opposite direction. He spun around, suddenly bathed in the blinding glare of headlights. He started to back off the road. The car halted at the curb.

"Stay right where you are, Prescott!"

A huge figure lurched from the car and strode into the bright beams. Recognition came slowly. Sylvester, the sheriff's deputy. Rosecreek had apparently decided to provide a token response to Gardner's plea on the phone.

"What's going on?" Gardner said.

"Jus' get in my car and everything'll be fine."

"*Your* car! Am I under arrest?"

"Wouldn't say that exactly. Now let's jus' move it."

"Look, check with Sheriff Rosecreek. He knows why I'm here."

"Already talked to him. Expect I'll be hearin' back shortly." Sylvester rested a big hand on his holstered gun. "For now, get in the car."

Gardner got in the car. Sylvester stood outside on the driver's side, elbow on the frame of the open door.

"A man was just inside the Welles's house," Gardner said. "He had a flashlight. He came running down through those trees. Did you see him?"

"I heard. That's all—*heard*." The inflection implied a more intimate suspicion.

"Christ, you don't think it was *me!*"

"Let's keep it easy."

"I heard his car, heard him streak away. Then he jammed on his brakes. And skidded, I think." Gardner felt a surge of hope. He pointed through the windshield. "Was a police car parked down there?"

"No use askin' questions, Prescott."

"But—"

"We'll *wait*."

After ten mute minutes, Sylvester emitted a small sigh and heaved his weight to the seat, leaving the door open. Gardner smoked his third cigarette, casting glances up at the dark house. Could the sheriff be inside? No—he would probably have snapped on some lights. The trespasser had left by the back door, which probably opened from the utility room. A natural exit; his car had been parked on the street below. He had doubtless entered the same way—the stolen front-door key must fit both locks.

A phone buzzed beneath the dash. Sylvester grabbed it, announced himself, and slid out to the road. He took a step away, stretching the cord, and cupped his mouth. Mostly he listened, occasionally nodding his huge head and interjecting a muffled yes or no. He climbed back on the seat and replaced the phone.

"The sheriff'll be 'long in a while."

What the hell was keeping him? Probably he had been off duty, sleeping, judging by the late hour, and had taken his time to wake up and dress. The thought crushed all hope that Tina's lover had been intercepted. If he had been, the sheriff would have stormed to the scene in minutes, escorting the handcuffed intruder to the premises. Gardner groaned with the bitterness of defeat. And apprehension.

Rosecreek drove up fifteen minutes later and parked facing Sylvester. In the reflections from the lights on the windshield, Gardner could not see his face clearly, only his big fawn-colored hat. He got out and Sylvester went to him. They spoke briefly, Gardner overhearing the sheriff say as they broke apart, "You two wait in front. I'll take the back door."

Presumably he planned either to pick the lock or use a skeleton key.

Rosecreek was standing in the open front door, lamps behind him lit, when Gardner and the deputy came through the gate.

"I understand you saw a light, Mr. Prescott, like a flashlight, in Catherine's room?"

"That's right. Then he came crashing down the bank. I heard him start his car, really rev it up, and take off." Gardner felt a necessity to be very specific, in case the skeptical sheriff should have any doubts. "Then—"

"Okay, I've got the picture." Rosecreek gave him a long, contemplative look. Gardner was reminded of a movie scientist attempting to penetrate the inner mysteries of a creature from outer space. "Show me the room," the sheriff said.

Gardner led them up to Catherine's room. Sylvester snapped on the overhead light and the bed lamp, then disappeared into the bare closet. Rosecreek started with the bureau, flinging open the empty drawers, running his hand around inside, and slamming them shut. Gardner stepped from his path as he approached the night table. Rosecreek pulled out the narrow drawer and sat on the bed to examine it. He felt it inside and out, shook his head, and prepared to slide it back. He stiffened. The drawer thudded to the carpet as he dropped to one knee and reached under the table. When he stood up he was clutching a folded yellow manuscript and a single piece of stiff white paper.

"Must have been jammed behind the drawer," he said.

Why had the man chosen that particular place? Gardner wondered. Perhaps because if Scott should for some reason return, it would not be to enter Catherine's room, let alone the drawer. But later, when someone else—the police or the new owners—opened the drawer, the evidence would immediately fall into their hands.

Sylvester had emerged from the closet and was slouching against the door frame. Gardner watched Rosecreek as he held the manuscript under the bed lamp, scanning the pages. Nothing he read changed his inscrutable expression. He tossed it on the bed and turned his attention to the white paper.

As he read, his jaw sagged and his equine eyes bulged. He jumped to his feet and waved the paper at Gardner.

"You're Welles's buddy, Mr. Prescott. Did he tell you anything about *this?*"

Gardner bristled. "How do I know when I haven't read it?"

Rosecreek thrust the paper at him.

Despite his familiarity with Tak's reported arrangements for flying Sinjuko to Scott, Gardner managed a more subdued version of the sheriff's astonishment. Finishing the letter and handing it back, he made his face go blank.

"Scott never said a word about this to me." The truth.

"Did his *wife* ever mention it to you?"

Gardner hedged. "Sheriff, it should be damned obvious who Tina's confidant was—the man whose child she was carrying when she was murdered."

Rosecreek worked his mouth as if to spit, but swallowed instead. "And you think the guy who was here tonight—"

"Then you agree that some *was* here?" Relief flooded through him.

"How can I think otherwise? Sylvester heard him."

"And I not only *heard* him, but *saw* him."

"Try not being so defensive, Mr. Prescott. I believe you. Why would you want to stick it to the very man you're so convinced is innocent? And why would you have called me in the first place to tell me about the key? Relax."

"I'm relaxed." He wasn't.

"Okay, the stuff was planted tonight, *had* to be because right after the murder we searched every inch of this house, including this room. So who did the planting?"

"Tina's lover, of course."

"It would look that way. But even so, that wouldn't prove he's guilty of murder. He could simply have been protecting himself by exposing the real murderer—Scott Welles."

"Oh, for God's sake! Can't you see it's a frame-up? How did he get the material if not from Tina? After killing her!" Gardner deliberately omitted the theft of the manuscript from the boat; it seemed only to confuse his case.

"She might also have given it to him some time before that night." Rosecreek rubbed his long chin reflectively. "The fact is we can't even be absolutely sure that the person who stashed this stuff *was* Mrs. Welles's lover."

Gardner gritted his teeth. "Next you'll be saying the butler did it."

"That's not such a joke. It could even be that Helen, the housekeeper, was mixed up in this. It shouldn't surprise you that she had a key to the front door."

"Wow! You can't really *believe* that!"

"All I'm saying is that we just can't settle that the guy who was here tonight murdered Tina Welles." He paused. "And we can't even be sure he was one of the men from the club—Crowley, Cornman, Spain."

Gardner slapped his forehead. He felt as if his brain was deliberately being bombarded with false signals to jam it. "Sheriff, you seem to be going miles out of your way to make this case one big confusing *mess!*"

"Oh, I'm not so confused, Mr. Prescott. We still have two fugitives. And one of 'em has a motive that's a cop's dream"—he waved Tak's letter, then shot a finger toward the manuscript—"a Japanese mistress secretly flown here from Tokyo just before Welles's wife was murdered!"

Carmel

1968

XXVI

Scott Welles smiled anxiously down on Catherine lying supine on the high black-leather couch.

"You know there's nothing to be afraid of," he said. "Just a very little sting, that's all."

From behind him, out of the cone of light from the tall table lamp, a gentle feminine voice said, "*Sukoshi*."

Catherine grinned. "Yes, *sukoshi*. Little. Like a tetanus shot. Only this one will put me to sleep."

"Yes," Scott said, "and you'll wake up feeling fine."

"It's all right," Catherine said. "I don't mind." She turned her head, blonde hair spilling off the couch, and made a beckoning gesture. In a moment she was looking up at the dark, luminous, almond eyes she had come to trust. "Will you stay until its over?"

"Oh yes, Catherine."

Catherine smiled happily. She reached up and touched with her fingertips the rounded cheeks, the straight, black, glossy hair. "I wish I was just like you."

"It is nicer, I think, to be blond."

"*Burondo*."

"*Hai. Burondo.*"

Amusement glimmered in the eyes of both of them. Using Japanese words was their little joke, especially when they were funny corruptions of the English equivalent.

Scott felt a tap on his shoulder and turned. Dr. Charles Rush held the hypodermic poised and was staring at the tip of the steel needle. He was a short, bony, gray man with a brush mustache and steel-rimmed glasses. For many years he had been Scott Welles's doctor and friend in San Francisco and was now semi-retired in Carmel, occasionally acting as a consultant. Scott gave Catherine's shoulder a squeeze and moved back.

"Miss Yamada?"

She joined Scott and the doctor bent toward Catherine. She stretched out her arm.

"Say 'One hundred,' Catherine."

As if playing a game Catherine said, "One hundred."

"Are you good at counting backwards?"

"I think so."

"When I tell you to, count backwards from one hundred."

The doctor inserted the needle into the soft skin of the upper arm. Quickly he secured it with adhesive tape.

With wan humor Catherine said, "*Sayonara.*"

The gentle voice replied, "*Sayonara.* And soon, *konnichi wa!*"

"Yes—hello."

Dr. Rush turned to Scott and nodded toward the lamp table. Scott stepped to it and snapped on a small, thin tape recorder. An ironic smile twisted the corner of his mouth as he noted again that it had been made in Japan.

"Now, Catherine, count backwards from one hundred."

Frowning in concentration, Catherine counted slowly. At ninety-six her voice faltered. She only half-completed ninety-five when the frown smoothed out and her eyelids closed. The sodium pentothal had taken effect.

The doctor waited a few seconds before saying, "Catherine, this is Dr. Rush. Can you hear me?"

"Yes, I hear you." Her voice had thickened slightly but the words were clear.

"You may open your eyes if you like."

She opened her eyes: twin china-blue searchlights and with no more expression.

"Your father would like to talk to you now, Catherine."

"Good."

"Please answer everything he asks you."

"Why, yes." A note of surprise.

Dr. Rush discreetly retreated and whispered to Scott, "I'll be in the next room. Call me when you're finished or if you think you need me. I'll be checking the time. Miss Yamada?"

They both went out, closing the door quietly.

Scott stepped to the couch. For a few moments he was silent, resisting a pang of guilt at her helplessness, so apparent in the sightless blue eyes. The guilt was routed by the hope that the suspense would at last be ended. For five days, ever since fleeing Sausalito, they had secluded themselves in the isolated Carmel cottage, waiting for the doctor to return from a fishing trip on Oregon's Klamath River. Late yesterday, Sunday, he had finally picked up his phone, expressing delight at the call. But when Scott had gone to see him and told him what he wanted done, the delight quickly changed to dismay, then to uncertainty at the absence of official sanction, finally to reluctant agreement.

Scott's lips now formed Catherine's name, but no sound came out. The word was strangled by the fear—which had been swelling daily to monstrous proportions—that Catherine's response would be a damning exposure of guilt.

He gave a dry cough. "Catherine?"

A ghost of a smile flitted across her mouth. "Hi," she said, the word sounding weirdly incongruous.

"Catherine, do you remember the night not long ago when I came home and found you sitting up in bed? You were hugging your big tiger and you were very upset."

A sharp intake of breath. "Yes, I remember." Fright gave her voice the wispy quality of a small child's.

"Do you remember *why* you were upset?"

A pause. Then, tensely, "Yes, I remember."

"Tell me why, Catherine."

Silence.

"It will help me very much if I know, Catherine. Take your time. Just tell it the way it comes to you."

Her eyes were now crowding the sockets. "I was in my bed, sleeping. No, just half-sleeping, I guess. It was only a little after nine. I'd heard a door opening downstairs before and I thought it was you and I wondered if you'd come to my room to say good night. You didn't and I began to feel, well, awfully alone and kind of sad. After a while, I decided to go down to the kitchen for some milk. You'd see me, I thought, and would take me up to bed and I wouldn't feel sad anymore. So I went down the stairs. But when I got to the bottom and went past the living room, you weren't there and Tina wasn't either. I heard voices back down the hall, from your study, and thought that was where you both were. But that seemed funny because Tina hardly ever went into your study."

Her head strained slightly from the couch, as if preparing to face a nightmare image.

"Anyway, I went to the kitchen and stayed there for a little while, hoping you'd come out. Then I got a glass of milk and brought it back with me. I stopped at the stairs, listening to the voices. But now they weren't like voices, just sounds, crazy sounds, like people in trouble . . ."

Her voice choked off.

"Go on, Catherine."

Her head rose higher, tiny cords appearing in her neck. "I . . . I walked down the hall to the study. The door was closed but I could see some light coming from underneath. I kept hoping it would open and you'd come out and everything would be all right. But all I heard were those sounds—big breaths, slapping, and someone, Tina, all excited, saying, 'Now! *Now!* over and over. I got awfully scared. I thought something terrible was happening and I didn't know what to do but I knew I had to look. I took hold of the doorknob and turned it very slowly and opened the door just a crack and . . . *oh no, no, no, I can't, I can't!*"

Her head fell back on the black leather. A pulse pumped in her white throat.

"Please, honey, try. But rest for a minute."

For about twenty seconds, only Catherine's rapid breathing broke the stillness.

"Mother was lying on the floor on her back with her arms around someone. A man. He was on top of her. They didn't have any clothes on. So I knew what they were doing. I wouldn't have been scared or mad . . . I *wouldn't*, honest I *wouldn't* . . . if the man had been you. But it wasn't, I could tell, it *wasn't* . . ."

"Who was it, Catherine?"

"I don't know. There wasn't much light and all I could see was his back. I didn't want to look anymore. I went up to my room and sat on my bed and drank some of the milk. It made me feel sick and I went into the bathroom and threw up. I poured the rest of the milk down the sink and washed the glass and came back and got into bed. My head was aching terrible. But I forgot about it when I heard the fighting start. They were yelling at each other, shouting nasty things. I began to think how awful it would be if you came home and found them like that. Maybe, I thought, if I went back downstairs and made a lot of noise in the kitchen—like slamming the refrigerator and dropping a glass—they'd hear me and stop and he'd leave. So that's what I started to do. But when I got to the bottom of the stairs I . . . I stopped for a minute and listened. Tina kept shouting something about a letter . . ."

"A letter? What did she say about it?"

"I'm not sure exactly. She was swearing at him. 'You damn fool,' I think she said, 'This letter is all we need. And maybe the . . . the manuscript.' Then she said, 'It's proof he brought this Japanese . . . Japanese *bitch*,' she said, 'over here and is living with her. We can get everything he's got.' "

"Do you remember what he said?"

"I think he said, 'I don't *want* what he's got!' Then the phone rang and I heard Tina answer it. She hung up in maybe ten seconds and then everything got quiet—I could hardly hear them talking. So I knew it was you who'd called, saying you were on your way home. I thought the fighting was all over, so I ran upstairs to my room. But I was still scared and I pulled the blanket over my head and pushed my face into the pillow. After a while—it seemed like a long time— I heard a car go by. I thought the man had gone and I felt better because you wouldn't find him here. But then . . . *ohhhh!* . . ." Catherine's hands darted up to cover her pale face.

"Then what?" Scott glanced miserably down at her. "*Then* what, Catherine?"

Catherine's arms dropped exhaustedly to her sides. "Then, pretty soon, the fighting started all over again. Tina was almost screaming. I jumped up and opened my door. Tina had stopped yelling and all I could hear were sounds, but different than the first time. Like people wrestling and things being knocked over. Then I heard this awful smashing sound, then a thud.

Then I didn't hear anything for a couple of minutes. I just stood at my door, I couldn't move. Then I heard a car start up. I got to my window and saw the car go past. Then . . . *oh God* . . ." She sat bolt upright, palms rubbing furiously against her thighs, eyes transfixed.

Scott's jaws constricted. He bit out: "Tell me what you did then, Catherine. *Please!*"

"I went downstairs again. Back to the study. Oh, I can't, *can't* . . ."

"You're almost there, honey. Now go into the study."

A strangled whisper: "I'm in the study. Blood. Mother's head is lying in it. It's running down her hair. She's dead, I know she's dead. I'm so awfully scared and my head hurts so. But I'm not sorry. That's what's so horrible—*I'm not sorry!*" She began to shake.

Scott leaned forward intently; now came the critical question.

"Did you see anyone besides Tina? A man?"

"No. Just Tina. Oh God, maybe it's not true. Maybe I'm dreaming. Maybe I'm having a nightmare. Maybe I'll wake up and you'll be there and everything will be all right again."

Scott put an arm around her rigid shoulders. His breathing was as rapid now as Catherine's.

"That's all it is, a bad dream . . . See, I'm dreaming I'm walking up the stairs . . . Now I'm dreaming ing in my bed . . . But I'm so scared. *Scared! Won't somebody help me! Oh God, oh God* . . ." She began to sway back and forth.

Scott put his other arm around her and held her close, feeling tears spurt against his chest. "It *was* just a dream, Catherine, that's all, only a dream, it's all right now."

Slowly she began to relax. She released a shuddering sigh. Then calmly she said, "Yes, a dream."

Scott pressed her back on the couch. After a while he heard the door open softly.

"Is it now finished, Scott?"

"Yes," he said, "that's all."

"The doctor, I will tell him."

He went to the table and snapped off the tape recorder.

XXVII

Sitting at a desk in the larger of the cottage's two bedrooms, Scott played the tape for the fifth time. The volume was turned low so that Catherine, resting quietly in the opposite bedroom, would not hear and be horrified by her own words. Soon, he hoped, after the threat had been removed, he would try to explain everything in a way she could accept.

But first the terrible drama had to have an ending.

Perhaps what he had written on the long yellow pad—laboriously transcribed from the slow-spinning tape—was the beginning of the end. At least, if accepted by the police—Dr. Rush would certify its authenticity—it should lift all suspicion from Catherine, as well as from himself.

Listening closely to the replay of Catherine's voice, he penciled in a few additions to the transcript for clarity. Satisfied that it was as close to verbatim as he would get it, he snapped off the whirring tape. Getting up, he took the yellow pad to an easy chair next to the window and, in a shaft of sunlight, reviewed Catherine's agonizing revelations.

The man must have arrived around nine o'clock, probably at Tina's invitation. Hearing them in the study, Catherine had come downstairs and witnessed them on the floor in a naked, climactic embrace. She retreated to her bedroom, drank the milk, got ill. Then the verbal fight. And: "Tina kept shouting something about a letter."

Tak's letter—delivered by Scott's secretary to his home along with a stack of business mail. And intercepted by Tina. He wondered if she had made a copy. Probably. If so, her lover had doubtless taken it, probably on the night of the murder. But the letter—or if not the actual letter, its contents—would be of no use to him. Rosecreek would be professionally concerned only with the fact that the man's violent presence in the study had been established by the tape.

Then Catherine's discovery of the body. How could anyone listening to her tortured account question her innocence, despite any negative prejudice induced by her retardation? And with the removal of all suspicion, there would be no danger of Catherine being confined to an institution. True, an investigation would surely disclose her affliction. But hadn't he always wanted it revealed, so that she could be accepted openly, hopefully with understanding, for the loving person she was?

It was imperative, he decided, that Sheriff Rosecreek hear the tape. But he was still not so certain of its power to convince that he was willing to bring it personally to the sheriff's office. Nor was he willing to play it over the phone and risk having the call traced. No, first he'd try reading the transcript to Rosecreek from a public phone, which at least would be more difficult to trace.

It was past six o'clock when he drove the red Rambler into a Standard station on the approach to the highway. Inside the booth, he dialed information, got the number, and dialed again.

The sheriff, a rumbling voice informed him, had just left for the day.

"Can you catch him? It's important."

"Sorry."

"This is Scott Welles calling. *Welles*. I'm the husband of—"

"Hold on!"

In a minute the sheriff was on, his voice gruff and disbelieving. "Welles? *Scott* Welles?"

"Yes. Sheriff, I've got something—"

"How do I know you're Scott Welles?" His throat sounded clogged.

Scott paused to think. "For one thing, you've got my thumbprint from a bookend."

"Okay. Also, the voice seems right. Where are you?"

"First you'll have to listen to me."

A pause. "Shoot."

"I think you'll want this taken down. Have you got a stenographer available?"

"Hang on."

Gardner heard him bark an order.

"Just keep talking, Mr. Welles."

"Sheriff, I'm about to read you something. It's a transcript of a tape recording made in the office of a reputable doctor. The person talking is Catherine, my daughter. She was totally unaware that she was speaking because she had been put to sleep by an injection of sodium pentothal, one of the so-called truth drugs."

Scott heard a click in the connection. The stenographer was on.

"Go on, Mr. Welles. You'll be quoting your daughter. Testimony—I *assume* it's testimony—taken while she was under the influence of a *drug*."

Rosecreek had to get that into the record, complete with his own discrediting taint.

Scott read the transcript slowly, enunciating carefully, halting midway to clang more quarters into the slot. Rosecreek interrupted only once—at the reference to the letter.

"Do you know the letter your wife was talking about?"

"I can't be sure."

"I don't accept that."

"I'm only asking you to accept what's on the tape. That should be enough."

When Scott had finished he said, "That's it. *Now* what do you think, Sheriff?"

Scott heard him say to the stenographer, "Got it?" And the masculine reply, "Yes sir."

Then, to Scott, "I think I'd better have the actual tape, Mr. Welles." His tone was no longer skeptical, simply noncommital.

"You don't believe the transcript?"

"I didn't say that. But you *could* have invented it."

"I've got just one tape. I won't risk sending it."

Oddly, Rosecreek did not press it. In the pause that followed, Scott had the sensation that his ear was receiving brain waves.

"Are you still on, Sheriff?"

"I'm on. Look, I've got to read this over, think about it. Let me call you back."

"I'll call *you* back."

Rosecreek gave a juicy chuckle. "Okay, it's your money. And from what I've heard from your former boss, Cornman, and a certain real estate broker, you've got plenty. Try me in an hour."

It seemed pointless to go back to the cottage and then return. Instead, avoiding the town, he drove to the ocean and parked under a gnarled cypress overlooking a white-sand beach. He watched the orange sun inching toward the sea. A *setting* sun, western, not the rising sun of Japan. Everything seemed unreal. He thought of Tina, of Sinjuko, and of Catherine, anguished by the ordeals that each, in her own way, had endured. Now there was some hope . . .

He left forty minutes later, this time moving down the coast and stopping at a Union station. He called the sheriff from the booth.

"All right, Mr. Welles. It looks to me like this transcript fits with some things I know."

"Then you believe it's the truth?"

"I've got to *act* like it is."

"What does that mean?"

"It means that I may be able to work out a plan for nailing your wife's murderer. God help me if I'm wrong. But you'll have to tell me where you're staying."

"Forget it."

"I expected that. Okay. But it won't work unless you play ball. So brace yourself—I'm going to tell you a few things."

As Rosecreek exploded what he knew, Scott felt his body go rigid, heard blood pulsing in his ears.

"My God," he muttered when the sheriff had finished.

"I know it's tough, Mr. Welles. A man you knew and I guess respected."

"Tina—with *him!* His marriage seemed so damned solid."

"Maybe it was. Maybe it still is. But some guys can't stand not having another thing going. Anyway, what I've given you is still circumstantial. I can't bet my badge on it. So the first thing we've got to do is get lover-boy out in the open. And the best way to do that is through Gardner Prescott."

"Gardner?"

"Yes. We've been tailing this guy and he's been sticking to Prescott like a second skin, thinking he knows something the police don't. I can't approach Prescott—he doesn't trust me and would suspect a trick. He can't be reached by phone, so I suggest you send him a wire. Just tell him that it's important that he call you and give him your number. When he hears your voice he'll know it's on the up and up. And he'll jump to help. He's been turning himself inside out to cover for you."

"I'm grateful for that."

"You should be, Mr. Welles. If it wasn't for him, we'd never have staked out your house the other night. And your wife's . . . *friend* . . . he'd be in the catbird seat. With you framed so tight you couldn't wriggle out."

"You mean those planted . . . *documents?*"

"Yes, the letter plus the manuscript. But mostly the *letter*—the one that seems to have you so tongue-tied and that may be none of my business." Rosecreek paused, waiting for a reply. "All right, send the telegram to Prescott in the morning."

"What do I tell him when he calls?"

"Practically nothing. He's a great one for charging off on his own and I can't take any chances on a slip-up. If he knew the guy was on his tail, he might get big ideas and do something foolish. Just say you've got some vital information he should know about."

"Okay. I hope he can stand the sudden shock."

"A damned pleasant shock. He's been after this character all along. If my idea works out, he'll enjoy seeing this cocksman smeared with enough guilt to satisfy the devil. And I expect to be enjoying it with him."

Scott gave a dry laugh. "It sounds like the county's too small for you, Sheriff. You should run for state office."

"I tried that once. I was licked by a fella named Jim Beam. But to hell with that, Mr. Welles. I'm afraid there's one more thing I have to ask you to do."

"Anything you say."

"There's a part of that tape I'd like clarified. It's a small thing, but sometimes small things can make a big difference."

Scott felt his heart sink. Once again Catherine would have to be brought to Dr. Rush.

"Can it wait till tomorrow? Catherine's pretty exhausted."

"Tomorrow's okay. In that case, tell Prescott to come down in the late afternoon or evening. We may need the time. Call me after you leave the doc's. This time collect. We'll go over all this again. Now will you tell me your address?"

"Sixty Sealane Road, Carmel. It's a rented cottage."

The sheriff repeated it and got the phone number. "I'll shoot my deputy down there first thing in the morning. Sylvester. He'll explain about the tape."

Scott now resolved the question that had been pressing on his mind. "I'll also tell you another thing. I wouldn't if you hadn't found Tak's letter."

Briefly he told the sheriff about Sinjuko.

There was a long pulsing silence.

He heard the sheriff clear his throat. Then, speaking quietly, Rosecreek said, "Mr. Welles, I can't very well arrest you for that."

Scott had hung up before he wondered if he was being far too trusting.

It was eight o'clock when he arrived back at the cottage. Opening the door, he was surprised to find no one there to greet him. Perhaps the back yard, he thought, although the sun had long since dropped behind the tall pines and the clearing lay in deep shadow.

Apprehension accompanied him through the kitchen and out the back door. The red-brick patio and the lawn beyond were uninhabited. Panic threatened as he strode back inside and down the short hall to the two bedrooms. Both doors were closed. He raised a hand to knock on Catherine's, then drew back. Early as it was, she was probably asleep, her frail body drained of energy by the ordeal in Dr. Rush's office. His fears began to subside. He turned and opened the door to the larger bedroom.

The drapes were drawn shut and it took a few moments for his eyes to adjust to the semi-darkness. He looked toward the vanity and his heart melted with pleasure as a familiar figure rose from the oval stool and gave a final pat to her black hair. He drew in a breath. The lustrous hair was swept up in the style of a geisha's, and she was wrapped in a yellow silk kimono.

In the partial light, he had only to half-close his eyes and see the Sinjuko of more than twenty years ago.

She stepped daintily forward, smiling. "*Komban wa*," she said softly.

The lining of his throat seemed to swell. Huskily he said, "And good evening to you."

An unconscious memory stirred, dissolving in a great wave of nostalgia. Instantly he was back in a wood-and-paper house, sitting on a tatami floor beside a battered desk, watching the glory of Sinjuko's eyes as she fondled the tickets that would take them to the inn in Nikko. He was a young man again, and, in the dim light, this lovely creature moving so shyly but purposefully toward him was the girl of eighteen whose only wish was for his happiness.

His arms went around her and he held her close to his thumping heart, his voice catching as he murmured, "Oh my dear, my dear."

Her delicate hands stroked his back and she brought her mouth up to the hollow of his throat, her breath coming fast and warm. He drew slightly away, touching her cheek, her hair, desire rising inside him like a scalpel that would excise the resistant sadness.

She started to speak but he placed his fingers gently on her lips, saying, "I think it's time for bed."

She looked at him for a long time, then grasped his hand, kissed it softly, and without speaking, turned away.

Undressing and slipping beneath the sheet, he could hear her moving about in the bathroom. He rolled to his side, facing the window, eyes beholding an imagined scene of wary lovers in a high hospital bed.

He was still like that a few minutes later when, behind him, he heard a rustle of silk. He did not identify the sound as a kimono dropping to the floor until he felt the bed sag and the naked, quivering body press against his back.

It was the way it had begun in the small, narrow room overlooking a pathetic vegetable garden.

XXVIII

"Hello, Scott?"

"Hi, Gardner. I see you got my wire."

"A few minutes ago. What's happening?"

"I've come up with something important."

"What?"

"Something I think will completely clear Catherine and me."

"Terrific!"

"I can't discuss it on the phone. Can you come here?"

"Glad to. I can leave right now."

"Thanks. Catherine and I have an appointment in a couple of hours and I don't know how long it will take, so better make it later."

"Sounds like you just invited me to dinner. Where are you?"

"We're in Carmel. Just stay on 101 South and you'll see the signs. It should take you less than three hours. The address is Sixty Sealane Road. Got it?"

"Got it. Sixty Sealane Road."

"Call me when you reach town."

Fog was rolling in from the sea when Gardner drove off shortly after four o'clock. But passing through San Francisco and approaching Highway 101, the sun broke through. Reaching Palo Alto, it was all blue sky. He took off his jacket, his sense of adventure sharpening, his blood beginning to race.

Through San Jose and down the one-street, sun-baked farm towns strung out like game pieces in the long valley—Morgan Hill, Gilroy, Prunedale. Past orchards of peaches, prunes, apricots, flat acres of sugar beets, onions, watermelons. Salinas—the "salad bowl" —with level fields of lettuce dotted with stooping Orientals and Chicanos. Then right, skirting Fort Ord, the low wooden barracks looking withered in the waning sun. On to the Monterey Peninsula— Steinbeck country—and the smell of salt and the sight of a calm, blue bay.

He was passing through the town of Monterey when a dark-blue car that he had only vaguely and occasionally noticed in his rear-view mirror suddenly reappeared as he swung around a corner. The sight triggered an apprehension. Was he being followed?

He pulled to the curb and braked. Behind, the dark-blue car swung abruptly into a gas station. Probably just imagination, Gardner thought, but anxiety lingered. He geared the Jag forward, relaxing only slightly when he cut through rolling, pine-wooded hills and no longer saw the car in the mirror.

He entered Carmel at twilight from the top of the main drag, Ocean Avenue, split by a lush center strip of firs and shrubs and sloping down to the sea. He drifted past crowds of summer tourists nosing at the windows of consciously quaint shops, until halted by a small dirt parking area facing a white beach. Not having seen a gas station, he turned around and doubled back up the opposite side of the avenue. Cresting a hill, he spotted a Shell sign and pulled in. After filling the tank, the attendant directed him to Sealane Road. Listening, Gardner gazed about, looking for the dark-blue sedan.

His eyes fell on a car parked in a side street across the avenue. Same dark-blue color and looked like the same make and model. No driver was at the wheel, but he could be hidden nearby. Paranoia, Gardner told himself as he left the gas station.

But the image of the car continued to barrel through his mind. As a precaution, he drove back to the parking area at the foot of Ocean Avenue, turned around and killed the engine. He smoked a cigarette to a stub and ground it out. The blue sedan had not appeared. Still cautious, he drove up Ocean for a short block, cut left into an arbored street, then right, then left again, coming to a stop. Still no car. Feeling disoriented, he started for Sealane Road.

Twenty minutes later, after twice getting lost, he located it: a patched blacktop road winding through a thick forest of cypress. It was not until then that he remembered Scott's suggestion that he telephone from town for guidance. He had been too preoccupied with what was probably no more than a figment. Still, he was wary. His destination was number 60, but he stopped at a rural mailbox labeled 52. Feeling foolish, he pulled off the road onto a trail apparently intended for horses, and parked in a small open area. Returning to the road, he looked back. His car was not visible.

Better to *feel* foolish, he thought, than *be* fooled. The man might be lurking somewhere behind him; might . . . *Christ!* He might have gotten Scott's address from the Shell attendant and driven directly there! He might have known all along what the incriminating evidence was that Scott now possessed and at this moment was attempting to remove it! It was crucial that Gardner get to a place where he could view Scott's cottage unseen.

Head down, hugging the side of the road, he checked off the mailboxes as he passed—54, 56, 58—60. It stood on a post beside a white-graveled driveway that ran straight ahead for a short distance, turned sharply to the left, and disappeared into the trees. He paused about ten feet away, then moved quickly off the road into the cover of the cypress. Working his way through the underbrush and thickly needled branches, he followed the discernible line of the driveway. After a few minutes, he stopped and pressed behind a tree trunk. Directly ahead rose a brown shingle-roofed cottage set in a clearing on a green flowered lawn. He took a breath, bent low, and moved closer.

Only a faint aura of light came from the house, which now appeared gray against the darkening sky. He squinted at his watch. Almost eight o'clock. Scott had expected him well before this and must be eyeing the phone impatiently. Or was he staring into the muzzle of a gun?

The thought, absurd as it seemed, forced a decision. He would have to try for a look inside.

Crouching low, he crept to the lawn. He threw himself flat on the cool grass and cocked an ear for some sound, perhaps an engine. There was only a lunar silence. He slithered to the corner of the house and sat for a moment leaning against it. Breathing shallowly, he started to edge along the flagstone walk at the rear.

Lights glowed from two rooms—one at the far end, no doubt a bedroom, and the living room, now just above his head. He rose and peered over the windowsill. The curtains were drawn tight. He stared gloomily at the white figured cloth, then started to lower his head. He stopped. Stared. At the bottom of the curtains was a triangular gap. No more than two inches at the base, but wide enough to accommodate an eye. He pushed his nose against the cold windowpane and fixed a one-orbed gaze on the opening. The scene came into focus.

Scott Welles and a woman, obviously Japanese, both shoeless and wearing kimonos, sat cross-legged on the carpeted floor, their profiles to the window. Between them a long, low coffee table supported a bottle, a matching pair of small, handleless white cups, and a squat shaded lamp.

Gardner studied the strange woman. She wore her jet-black hair piled high, exposing delicate ears, and the nape of her neck curved gracefully from the yellow frame of her kimono neckline. Her cheeks were dark hollows in the pale-orange lamplight, but what he could see of her face appeared dusted lightly with powder, and her lips bore a trace of lipstick. She turned her head for a moment, giving a glimpse of penciled eyebrows and doe-like eyes with mascaraed lashes, a slant of it at the outer corners, as if proudly accentuating their Oriental cast. She was small and, Gardner surmised, perfectly formed, but any doll-like quality was dispelled when she reached for the bottle with graceful, flowing movements and poured what presumably was sake.

Scott raised his cup toward her and she solemnly clicked hers against it. Smiling, he said something to her—a single word. Gardner read her lips as, half giggling, she repeated the word—*"Kampai"*—the Japanese toast. She drank, her eyes over the rim adoring. Then she reached across and traced with her fingertips the firm line of his jaw, the ridged cheekbones, the short, straight nose, finally caressing his hair. Scott moved around the coffee table to her side. He put down his cup, bent, and kissed her throat, then raised his head slightly, pausing as if inhaling her scent.

Gardner jerked his head back, aware that he was acting no differently than a voyeur. It was embarrassingly clear that neither Scott nor Sinjuko was in immediate jeopardy, except perhaps from Catherine coming in unannounced from the bedroom.

He was convinced now that the suspected stalker existed only in fantasy. He was equally convinced that this was hardly the moment to break in on Scott. Nevertheless . . . He rose and circled toward the front of the cottage. Then he sucked in an enormous, gaping gasp as his head suddenly exploded into a universe of lights, followed instantly by a blackness that was absolute.

XXIX

Consciousness was at first a pounding against the temples. Then . . .

"Easy, Gardner. Don't try to move."

Scott.

"Scott, what the hell . . ." He gave his head a shake, feeling his cheeks part from the bones. Pain shot through his skull but his brain began to clear.

"You got clobbered," Scott said grimly.

Gardner reached to the top of his head and felt a handkerchief sticky with blood. Removing it gingerly, he explored his scalp with his fingertips. A gash, less than an inch long, blood oozing through his hair. Memory rushed back.

"I . . . I parked some distance back because I thought I'd been followed. Then I walked to your mailbox and came part way up the drive." He could not bring himself to say that he had reached the house. "I wanted to see if someone had beat me here. What brought you out here?"

"I heard the crunch of gravel and opened the door to look. No one was there. I went back into the house but started to get jumpy, worried you hadn't arrived. So I went outside again, this time with a flashlight, and there you were, flat on your back."

Gardner quickly told him of the stop to get directions at the gas station and forgetting to telephone. "He could have gotten the address from the attendant. But when he saw me pull into the woods, he decided to see what I had in mind. Probably followed me on foot."

Scott helped him to his feet. "Come on, let's get inside and clean up that gash. I'll explain everything over a stiff drink."

Several lamps were now lit in the living room but no one was there. Scott led him down the short hall to the bathroom. The two doors flanking it were closed and Gardner heard no sound. He swabbed away the blood with a washcloth and applied an antiseptic.

Gardner was still slightly giddy when he came in and eased down on the sofa. From beyond an open swinging door off to the left, Scott could be heard prying at a stuck ice tray. He swore. Gardner decided to hear Scott's news before taking up time with the story of the stolen key, the witnessed interloper, the discovery of the manuscript and Tak's letter, Rosecreek's obfuscating rationales that still left the burden of guilt on Scott. Meanwhile . . .

"I didn't know you owned a secret hideaway down here, Scott."

"I don't own it. It's rented."

"Wasn't that risky, giving your name to a rental agent?"

"I had someone else handle it."

"He's trustworthy, I hope."

The plop of an ice cube.

"Completely. But it's a she, not a he. I've known her since she was a teen-ager. We came in her car. I sold mine to a used car dealer. Practically gave it away."

"She lives in Carmel?"

The gurgle of whiskey.

"No, San Francisco. Matter of fact, I once told you about her uncle."

"I don't recall."

"A buddy of mine in the Occupation. You couldn't forget his name. George Washington Takimoto.

My God!

"He's her *uncle*? What's her *name*?"

"Yamada. Suzuki Yamada. Suzie. She's a schoolteacher, off for the summer. She was born here, same as Tak. Her mother, Tak's sister, still lives in Salinas."

S. Yamada—that's all it had said in the little metal frame above the doorbell. Was that where Scott had brought Sinjuko for sanctuary?

Or had Sinjuko never arrived?

Was the Japanese woman he had seen with Scott in Sausalito—the woman behind one of those closed bedroom doors—Suzuki Yamada?

Scott came in, swinging the door closed behind him. He thrust out a drink. Gardner stared at the glass, more deeply stunned than he had been by the blow on the head.

"Anything wrong, Gardner? You look like you're having a relapse."

"No. No. I guess I'm still worried about that goon." He took a gulp of the drink. "Go ahead. Tell me what you've got."

All thought of Suzuki Yamada vanished when Scott said, "Rosecreek planned this. He knew you'd be tailed."

"What!"

"Yes, but only because I'd called him. I—"

He was interrupted by a squeaking noise. His head went up.

Gardner was on his feet, gripping his glass as if prepared to use it as a weapon. Suddenly he relaxed. He smiled.

Catherine came shuffling down the hall, sleepily lovely in pink silk pajamas. She smiled wanly and ran fingers through her long blonde hair.

"What are *you* doing up?" Scott said. Exasperation tinged his voice.

"I'm sorry. But I heard doors opening and closing

and heard you in the driveway. I thought something might be wrong."

Gardner wondered if the Japanese woman in the other bedroom was also awake.

"Nothing's wrong, Catherine," Scott said.

"I'm glad." She came forward and shook hands with Gardner. "Hello, Mr. Prescott, it's nice to see you."

Before Gardner could reply, Scott said gently, "Now back to bed with you." He hugged her with one arm, turning her half around. As she left, he gave her bottom an affectionate spank.

When he heard her door close, he said rapidly, "Yesterday I took Catherine to a doctor. He injected her with sodium pentothal, a truth drug. While she was in a trance, I questioned her." He drew a reel from his pocket. "It's all recorded on this tape."

"But what's this about Rosecreek?"

"You'll understand better after you hear the tape." He strode to a small machine atop a low bookcase just outside the kitchen door. Threading the tape, he said, "I'll keep it low, so Catherine won't hear. She'll be asleep in a few minutes."

Gardner settled himself on the sofa and lit a cigarette.

Scott pressed a button and remained bent over the recorder. There was a whir of leader tape. He straightened, facing Gardner and resting an elbow on the bookcase.

"Now, Catherine, count backwards from one to a hundred."

"One hundred . . . ninety-nine . . . ninety-eight . . . ninety-seven . . . ninety . . . six . . . ninety . . ."

As the tape progressed, with Scott gently questioning and Catherine answering in an ethereal voice that peaked at times to terror, Gardner's muscles tightened, his breathing quickened. A long ash dropped from his cigarette. He turned his back to

Scott and closed his eyes, projecting the drama on his brain as if on a movie screen.

He saw Catherine go down the stairs for a glass of milk . . . pause to listen to the voices in the study . . . return from the kitchen . . . stop, transfixed by the sounds of animal ecstasy . . . slowly turn the doorknob to the study . . .

"He was on top of her. They didn't have any clothes on. So I knew what they were doing . . ."

Saw her run upstairs and get sick . . . come back down . . .

"She was swearing at him. 'You damn fool,' I think she said, 'this letter is all we need . . . the manuscript.' Then she said, 'It's proof he brought this Japanese . . . Japanese bitch,' she said, 'over here and is living with her. We can get everything he's got.'"

So Scott knew that Tina had intercepted Tak's letter.

"I think he said, 'I don't want what he's got!'"

Rejection. The first step toward violence.

". . . the phone rang and I heard Tina answer it. She hung up in maybe ten seconds . . . So I knew it was you who'd called, saying you were on your way home."

Gardner turned his head and looked at Scott. His expression was blank.

"After a while—it seemed like a long time—I heard a car go by. I thought the man had gone and I felt better because you wouldn't find him here. But then . . . ohhh!"

Low as the volume was, Catherine's wail struck Gardner like a scream tearing through a hushed theater. The horror it implied overrode the words that immediately followed. His ear picked up isolated phrases.

". . . awful smashing sound . . . I couldn't move

... heard a car start up ... saw the car go past. Then ... oh God ..."

A few seconds of whirring tape.

"Turn that damned thing off! Now!"

Every muscle in Gardner's body constricted. The voice, hard and deep, had not come from the tape.

Gardner heard the click of a button. Then dead silence. Like a man favoring an injured back, he pivoted slowly around.

Scott stood stiff as a plank, his hands, fingers spread, held away from his sides. Behind him, the swinging door to the kitchen stood partly open. Out of the darkness protruded a blacksleeved arm. At the end of the arm glittered a gun. The man pressing the muzzle against the back of Scott's head, prodding him into the room, was Phipps Spain.

XXX

Phipps Spain said, "Let's keep this nice and quiet, Scott." He glanced toward the hall. "Unless you want your daughter to join the fun."

Scott nodded stiffly, as though partially paralyzed.

"Now rewind the tape and hand it to me. Turn the volume to zero."

With robotlike movements Scott turned the volume knob, reversed the tape, waited until it had whirred to the leader, then snapped off the reel. He handed it to Phipps, who dropped it into his jacket pocket.

"Go to the sofa and sit next to Prescott."

Scott crossed the room woodenly and placed himself down. Gardner, until then too petrified to move, slid over slightly. Staring up at the tall, dark figure grimly pointing the gun, it was impossible to imagine him as the bantering, hail-fellow-well-met man who fondly called his wife Charley. He must have entered the kitchen through a door from the garage. Gardner's feelings were strangely ambivalent—fear for his own and Scott's safety, relief that Tina's lover had at last been revealed. All the evidence against Phipps Spain began to fall into place in Gardner's mind, along with a sense of the outrageous irony of the situation. Damn that stewbum Rosecreek! Where was he?

He burst out: "You stole the key! You planted the letter and manuscript in Catherine's room! You—"

"Damned right I did. I thought it was time the police had concrete evidence against this bastard."

Gardner said quickly to Scott, "I was going to tell you about it. He tried to frame you."

Scott said nothing. His eyes were on the gun.

Phipps shrugged off the charge. "The painful fact is, it didn't work. You got to them first."

"*I* got—?" Gardner's mouth snapped shut. It might be better if Phipps didn't know they were in Rosecreek's possession.

"You took them as soon as I left the house that night. Coming down the bank, I saw a car parked off the road. I didn't think much about it until the other day when I spotted what looked like the same heap up on the marina. You got into it."

"So you've been following me all along."

"I had some professional help. But I took over full time after placing the car, and that night checking the house. The priceless items, need I say, were gone. Everything fit when that Western Union kid boarded the boat this morning and you beat it to a phone. Scott gets word to you to phone him, maybe for no other reason than that he's climbing the walls and thinks the police might have told you something. You tell him you've got the manuscript and the letter from his army buddy—real gas chamber evidence. He says to hurry on down."

"You're dead wrong."

"But you didn't just drive up and knock on the front door. No, you hid the car in the woods and sneaked up to the back of the house." Phipps gestured toward the rear window. "You spent quite a while spying through those curtains."

Scott gave a start. He suddenly flushed as he eyed Gardner inquiringly. Gardner was speechless. But his face, he knew, was stamped with guilt.

"Now that seemed damned peculiar," Phipps said. "At the moment, all I could think of was that you planned to try your hand at blackmail. You seem like a guy who can use a little cash and those papers are worth a lot to Scott. Anyway, I figured you were checking the house to make sure no one was inside who might block the deal."

More for Scott's sake than Phipps's, Gardner said, "I thought I'd been followed. I wanted to be sure he—*you*, as it turns out—hadn't gotten here ahead of me."

"That finally occurred to me. But only after I'd started searching you."

"And you didn't find the papers. Because I didn't have them."

"Stop it, Prescott. I didn't find them because my search didn't get very far. I was scared away by Scott. But I know those papers are here. You've delivered them to Scott. They're here in the house and I want them."

Scott spoke for the first time. "Forget it, Phipps. They're not here. Gardner brought me nothing. Why not settle for the tape?"

Phipps's mouth curled in a smile. "Scott, you seem to think this tape nails me to the wall. The fact is, if it ever got into court—and I don't intend that to happen—it could *help* me. Sure it alleges that someone—*someone*—was having a roll in the study with Tina. There are, I regret to say, a number of guys who might qualify for that role. But even if that someone proved to be me, it shows that I turned her proposition down flat. You heard the tape: 'I don't *want* what he's got!'—that's what the man said. The gospel straight from your daughter's lips."

"The tape also reported a furious argument, Phipps."

"You bet there was an argument! She was turning the pressure on me full blast. She'd been hounding me to marry her for months. I held her off, saying we'd live like paupers. Then she found out she was pregnant. She couldn't pass that off on you because of that little tie-off job you had performed. She was about to settle for an abortion when she learned about your long-loved Japanese girl friend. Eureka! Now she could stick it to you and get all your dough and I'd rush to share the wealth. She thought wrong. I already *have* a wife. And, believe it or not, I love her. A pleasant little side arrangement, fine. But marriage—I wasn't having any. So she blew her stack. And I blew mine. And that's all you can hang on me."

In desperation Gardner said, "The very fact you faked an alibi to cover the time of the murder proves your guilt. You saw to it that you were signed out of your office at ten-forty."

"Hell, yes! When I spotted the item about Tina's death in the paper the next morning I whipped into the office and added my name to the list. I had to protect myself." He waved the gun impatiently. "But even if everything I did is established beyond doubt, it's not going to clear you, Scott. Not when the police read that great love story you authored and the letter that brought it all up to date. What better motive could a man have for killing his wife, especially when she'd been hanging on to him simply as a meal ticket? And," he added nastily, "balling every guy she could drag into the bushes."

Scott started up as if to spring, his face flaming with fury. "Goddamn you, there's no manuscript, no letter here!"

Phipps aimed the gun at Scott's chest bone. "The gentleman doth protest too much."

Scott dropped back, clenching and unclenching his fists.

"Sheriff Rosecreek has those documents," Gardner finally said.

Phipps gazed at him sardonically for a few seconds. "Well, well, aren't you the bright boy. Suppose you tell me about it."

Haltingly, sensing that his every word lacked conviction, Gardner related the circumstances leading to the discovery of the papers.

"Nice try, Prescott. So those two cops just happened to be passing by?"

"No," Gardner said wearily, "I'd called Rosecreek earlier about the missing key."

"Sorry, friend, it's too convenient. I don't buy it." His eyes glazed over in thought. "I'm afraid I have to try another tack. Prescott, stand up and turn your back to me."

Gardner glared at him for a moment, then pushed to his feet and turned around. Looking down at Scott's face, he saw an expression of bemusement slowly turning to fear.

"Now, Mr. Prescott, I want you to walk down that hall and bring back Catherine."

Scott leaped to his feet. "For God's sake, Phipps!"

"Scott, I swear it, I'll blow this man's brains out if you say another word. Sit down."

Scott sank to the sofa.

"Prescott, I'll be here with Scott. You try to be a hero and it will be *his* brains."

Half-dazed, Gardner shambled down the hall. Reaching Catherine's door, he opened it quietly, leaving it ajar as he stepped inside. The wedge of light from the hall illuminated Catherine's blond hair fanned out on the pillow. He gave her shoulder a gentle shake. She rolled lazily to her back. The whites of her eyes flashed.

"I'm sorry to wake you, Catherine."

"Oh! It's Mr. Prescott."

"Yes. I don't like to disturb you, but you're wanted in the living room."

"That's all right." She threw back the blanket and slid her bare feet to the carpet. She adjusted her pink pajamas, then smoothed her hair. She rose and preceded Gardner out the door.

Scott stood facing them as they entered, Phipps behind him, the gun not visible.

"Phipps," Scott said in a tortured voice, "this has gone far enough!"

"Not yet it hasn't." Phipps stepped back to the center of the room. "Catherine, come here."

Eyes rounded in fear, arms pressed to her sides, she moved like a sleepwalker and stood next to him. Phipps swung the gun to within six inches of her head.

"Now, Prescott, get the Japanese woman."

"Phipps," Scott said, "there's no one else in this house."

"Oh no? What'd you do, fly her in just for the weekend? You're a liar. Prescott, get moving!"

Gardner was back in seconds, his expression faintly smug. "Scott was telling the truth. There's no one there."

For an instant Phipps looked disconcerted. "I'm afraid I can't take your word for it. Maybe there's a more reliable source." He reached out and lifted Catherine's chin, staring intently into her white face.

"Catherine, you wouldn't want me to hurt anyone, would you?"

Her lips trembled. "No."

"Then you'd better tell me. Is the Japanese woman—Sinjuko—in the bedroom?"

"Sinjuko?"

"Yes." He flourished the gun. "Answer me, Catherine. Is she there?"

She looked in confusion at Scott.

"No," Catherine said.

"Good coaching, Scott." Phipps bent his face close to Catherine's. For a few instants he studied her eyes, as if examining them for truth. His glance shifted to calculate Scott. Releasing Catherine's chin, he rubbed his fingers nervously against his thumb, his face reflective.

"These days you just can't trust anyone. I'm afraid I'll have to make a personal inspection. You lead the way, Catherine."

Scott jerked forward.

"Hold it, Scott. If you and Prescott behave yourselves, Catherine won't be harmed. If you don't . . ."

Scott pulled back.

Catherine walked stiffly from the room, the gun leveled at her back, as Phipps followed.

Gardner and Scott waited in tense silence. A long minute passed. Phipps's muffled voice, guttural as the growl of an animal, echoed from the bedroom.

"Goddamn it," Scott said, "I'm going in there."

Footsteps sounded before he could move. Catherine, head bowed, approached ahead of Phipps. She wiped at her eyes with shaking fists. Oh God, thought Gardner, she's about to break down.

Phipps Spain seemed to be undergoing some strange transformation. The gun, though still aimed at Catherine, was held loosely. His jaw had gone slack. His eyes darted back and forth between Catherine and the garment he carried over his left arm.

It was a yellow silk kimono, and clutched in his hand was an amorphous black mass.

Catherine ran to Scott and buried her face against his chest. Gardner heard him take a shuddering breath.

Phipps veered into the room and faced them. "I thought she might be hiding in the closet. She wasn't. These *were*."

Scott's face was still as stone.

"A kimono," Phipps said. He shook it to the floor. "And this," he added, dangling the black shape from his fingertips. "A wig."

A breathless pause.

"Catherine, lift up your head."

Slowly she raised her head.

Gardner looked at Catherine. Tears streamed down her cheeks.

"Look closely, Mr. Prescott."

Dark tears.

"Careless child," Phipps said, "she didn't wipe off all the mascara."

Gardner felt a foreboding.

"And in the bedroom—*Scott's* bedroom—I asked her a question. I asked her if she'd slept in that bed."

No! Christ, Scott, no!

"She looked at the gun and said . . . *yes!*"

Gardner stared in horror at Scott, whose face could have belonged to a corpse. Except for the eyes, now staring past Phipps.

He barely heard Phipps Spain say with malicious triumph,

"That beats everything! Scott Welles screwing his own kid!"

There were five heartbeats of silence.

"Drop it, Spain, or I'll empty this gun."

The gun, a forty-five, was jammed against the back of Spain's neck. Gripping it, finger taut on the trigger, was the big right hand of Sheriff Rosecreek.

XXXI

Phipps slowly spread his fingers and the gun thudded to the floor. Scott retrieved it and handed it to Rosecreek, who dropped it into his empty holster.

Phipps shook himself like a drenched dog and turned to face the sheriff. "That gun of yours should be aimed at Welles, not me."

Rosecreek produced handcuffs from the back pocket of his khakis.

Phipps backed off, flapping the wig at Catherine. "There's your motive for murder. His daughter! *She's* the reason Welles killed his wife!"

Gardner and the sheriff stared at Scott whose haggard face bore a look of resignation. He tightened his arm around Catherine's quivering figure.

"Catherine is *adopted*," he reminded them harshly. "And she is not a child. She is a *woman*, with all the feelings of a woman."

The word inspired a look of defiance on Catherine's face. Her delicate chin came up as she said. "I'm twenty-three years old. Tina never wanted anyone to know, because of the accident and what it did to me. But *I* knew. And now Tina's dead."

"I told her about Tina yesterday," Scott said. "After we came from the doctor's. I should have told her in the beginning." The pain had dissolved from his face and he glanced down at Catherine with love.

Contemplating her flushed face, Gardner realized that she was indeed a woman, one who had come of age in a single giant leap. Filtering through his stupefied mind was the thought that both of them had at last escaped from a world of hypocrisy and deceit and undeserved shame. A question pushed the thought aside:

"Where is the . . . the woman who drove you here?" He could sense Rosecreek and Spain sharing his goggle-eyed wonder.

"Suzie Yamada?" Scott said. "She's in Salinas visiting her mother. It's just a short ride. She took the bus yesterday afternoon." His eyebrows rose as he grasped what was in Gardner's mind. "She's an old friend. She'd often drive out to Sausalito and stop on the pier to watch Catherine fish. And sometimes I was her purchasing agent—stuff she wanted to send to her Uncle Tak."

Sheriff Rosecreek looked like an elderly Indian chief trying vainly to understand the mysterious ways of the white man.

"Suzie gave me the wig and the kimono," Catherine said. She flashed Scott an adoring glance and added ingenuously, "she knows I like to make believe I'm Japanese."

Scott's "lovely geisha," Gardner thought, remembering what Tina had heard in the study.

Phipps, whose eyes had not strayed from Rosecreek's gun, but had been absorbing everything with a puzzled scowl, now challenged Scott. "This is all very damned touching. But what about your Japanese girlfriend, the one you flew here from Tokyo? Or did you cancel her out when you found you had something pretty luscious right in your own house?"

Anger flared in Scott's eyes, replaced by disdain. "I did not bring Sinjuko to this country. I sent Tak money so that she could fly to Switzerland. She had tuberculosis, had it since late in forty-seven. I never knew until Tak found out several weeks ago and wrote to me. By then, she was only half-alive. The best doctors for that kind of thing, I learned, are in Zurich. So that's where she went."

There was a deep silence. Sheriff Rosecreek, for once, did not seem at all surprised, but Gardner's head was reeling. Catherine . . . *not* Sinjuko! Sinjuko . . . a lovely young girl in some old photographs and a yellowing manuscript. Nothing more. Oh Tina, poor, tragic Tina. . . .

Phipps broke the silence by flinging the wig to the floor. "But you've still got a motive and she's standing right beside you, in spite of all your sanctimonious good samaritan crud! Believe me, Sheriff, when I left Tina that night she was as alive as you are. The only one who could have seen her before she was murdered was Welles. We all know he left the office in time to do the job."

The outburst alerted Rosecreek, who strode quickly to Phipps and snapped on the steel handcuffs. "I'm afraid, Spain, that you talked too much while I was behind that door."

"For chrissakes, Sheriff, just what *did* you hear? That I was sleeping with Tina? That I got her pregnant? That I told her to get lost? There's not a goddamn thing you can charge me with!"

"I wouldn't say that, Spain. For openers, I can charge you with illegal entry and attempted murder."

"You mean because I was waving a gun around? Christ, that was nothing but a bluff and you know it. I had to get those papers and that damned tape."

"Which I'll take back now, thanks," said Rosecreek, lifting the reel from Spain's pocket. "After you." He prodded him to the front door with his gun and turned to Welles. "I've got Sylvester waiting outside. He'll take Spain in. I'll brief him and be back shortly so we can play the rest of the tape. Meanwhile"—he nodded toward Catherine—"you'll probably want to get her settled down." He marched a muttering Spain out the door.

Sitting on the sofa while Scott led Catherine down

the hall to the bedroom, Gardner thought about the astonishing relationship between the two. At first so shocking, it now struck him that it had a peculiar, almost inexplicable rightness about it. They had so much unselfishly to give each other. Scott could give her more than joy, more than companionship, more than a feeling of security. He could also give her what must seem like a miracle—self-fulfillment. And she could give him all these things, plus a renewal of the values abandoned so long ago. But how racked with guilt Scott must have been, and how relieved he must now be to have it all out in the open at last.

Scott returned quickly, his face reminding Gardner of an infantryman he had seen pulled from combat in Korea. Expression blank. Eyes sightless. Nature's mask for a terrible inner turbulence.

"My God, Scott, was I ever wrong about you! I was convinced you'd flown Sinjuko over here. We *all* were. Rosecreek, Spain, and—" He broke off abruptly.

"And Tina," Scott finished for him. "So you knew about it all the time. Lord, I wish you'd brought *everything* up right after Tina died. I'd have straightened you out fast, and you'd probably have felt a lot more justified in your support."

"Not really. For one thing, I saw no reason to embarrass you, especially when it wouldn't change things one way or the other. And since you'd practically bared the rest of your soul to me, I figured that if you wanted to keep *that* part of your life separate from the rest of the mess, who the hell was I to rake up more complications?

"Anyway, it doesn't matter now!" Gardner continued jubilantly. "It's *over*, Scott. Thank God, there's nothing more to worry about!"

Scott passed a hand across his eyes. "It's not finished yet, Gardner. Rosecreek will be back in a few minutes to play the rest of that tape, and—"

"And—?" Gardner froze.

"He'll also play the tape from Catherine's second sodium pentothal session with Dr. Rush. This morning. I'll explain fast," said Scott as he headed for the kitchen, "but I think we'd both better have a drink."

XXXII

Their glasses were empty when the sheriff returned. As he strode in, Gardner observed his flinty face, his big hand resting on the holstered gun, and rose with a feeling of anticipation.

Rosecreek cleared his throat and reached into his pocket. "Mr. Welles, now I'd like you to play this tape."

He handed the reel to Scott, who went to the recorder and stood there stiffly.

"Mr. Prescott, I'd appreciate it if you'd sit on the sofa."

Gardner complied, feeling as if he were entering a witness box. Rosecreek adopted a spread-legged stance between Scott and the front door, his profile to Gardner.

"Mr. Welles, if you'll start the tape just before the phone call, we'll have all we need."

Scott punched a button and the tape sped forward, screeching comic gibberish. He punched another button and it halted.

"Now go ahead," Rosecreek said. "But stop it when I give the word."

Gardner slid to the edge of the cushion. Scott pressed the button.

"'. . . don't want what he's got!' Then the phone rang and I heard Tina answer it. She hung up in maybe ten seconds and then everything got quiet—I could hardly hear them talking. So I knew it was you who'd called, saying you were on your way home."

"Stop!"

A click and instant silence.

Rosecreek let it drag on before saying, "Mr. Welles, the firm you worked for has its own building. That makes it easy to check on incoming and outgoing telephone calls." He paused. "On the night your wife was murdered, not a single telephone call was made from that building after six-thirty. So you could not have called from the office. Except in the afternoon, when you told your wife you'd be working. Is that correct?"

"Yes."

"And, that evening, you didn't telephone from anyplace else. Right?"

Scott breathed out heavily. "Yes, that's right."

"Therefore Catherine only *assumed* the call was from you. In fact, it came from somebody else." Rosecreek took a breath. "Okay, that's point number one. Now let the tape run some more."

"I thought the fighting was all over, so I ran upstairs to my room. But I was still scared and I pulled the blanket over my head and pushed my face into the pillow. After a while—it seemed like a long time— I heard a car go by. I thought the man had gone and . . ."

"Stop."

Rosecreek reflectively rubbed a silver sideburn with the heel of his hand. "So Catherine was in her room, her hearing muffled, for what 'seemed like a long time'—her words." He narrowed his eyes on Scott. "How long? What did she say when she was questioned again, Mr. Welles?"

"She wasn't sure but she seemed to think about twenty minutes."

"About twenty minutes. The man she had heard talking could have left a *few* minutes after she pulled the blanket and pillow around her head. She wouldn't have heard him go out the door or drive away. Then—let's say twenty minutes later—she came out from under the blanket and heard a car go by. She said, when she was questioned this morning, that she heard it on the street below her rear window. Now the question is—was that car *leaving* the house, or was it *coming to* the house? I say it was *coming to* the house."

Gardner said, "If it was coming to the house, wouldn't Catherine have heard him come in the front door?"

Rosecreek regarded him condescendingly. "Not likely, Mr. Prescott. At that point her door was closed. Mr. Welles, will you turn off the volume and skip to Catherine in the study."

Scott did as instructed, the tape whirring wordlessly.

"*. . . the fighting started all over again. Tina was almost screaming. I jumped up and opened my door. Tina had stopped yelling and all I could hear were sounds, but different than the first time. Like people wrestling and things being knocked over. Then I heard this awful smashing sound, then a thud. Then I didn't hear anything for a couple of minutes. I just stood at my door, I couldn't move. Then I heard a car start up. I got to my window and saw the car go past.*"

"Stop."

The tape snapped off.

Rosecreek scratched his crotch. "Okay. What've we got? A phone call. A reasonable assumption the man in the study—Spain, he admits it—left only minutes later. Twenty minutes after that, the sound of a car, which I claim was *approaching* the driveway. Then the fight—and the murder. Finally, a car gunning past the rear of the house, going *away*."

Gardner said, "So you're suggesting that Tina had *two* visitors that night."

"I am." Rosecreek stretched his long face, as if to relax its tension. "Let's put it together. First, the phone call. Mrs. Welles takes it and maybe writes down the number on a pad, saying she'll call back. Anyway, we found a phone slip that night—it was on the desk—and got a listing on the number. But when we located the phone, the call didn't seem a damned bit suspicious. I forgot about it—or almost. Now point number two."

Rosecreek turned to Gardner. "The section you'll hear now was spliced into Catherine's original tape. It's lifted from what she said under sodium pentothal during the *second* session. It clarifies something that had been bugging me."

He strode over to the machine and stabbed the button. Scott's voice rose from the tape.

"Catherine, you said you went to the window and saw the car go past. Do you remember that?"

"Yes, I remember."

"Did you get a good look at it?"

"Oh yes. It went under a street light."

"Can you describe it?"

"Sort of. It was a black convertible and it had a long front."

"Had you ever seen it before?"

"I don't know. Why, yes! I saw it in the driveway one day just before we left. I was coming back with Helen from playing. It was the day Mr. Prescott was with you."

The click of the stop-button resounded through the room like a gunshot.

Rosecreek pivoted on his heel and said to the shattered figure on the sofa. "The number we took from the pad was listed for the phone booth on your marina, Mr. Prescott. I see it this way. You called Mrs. Welles while she was wrangling with Spain. She said she'd call back in a few minutes. When she did, right after Spain left, she asked you to come over right away. You raced to the house and practically ran into

242

a buzz saw. That's when the wrestling started with things being knocked over and the smashing sound and the thud. You smashed Tina Welles with the bookend, ran out, and streaked back to the marina. But you weren't sure if she was dead. So you called from that same phone booth. You got Scott Welles. He told you his wife had been murdered."

Rosecreek paused. "The murderer has to be you or Mr. Welles. The evidence says it's you."

Gardner was hunched up as if tensed against the cold. Scott's words, when they had been alone, flashed through his mind: "God how I wanted to erase that tape. But I couldn't. Sylvester was there."

"Gardner, you poor bastard," Scott said wretchedly. "I'm so sorry . . ."

Gardner closed his eyes.

"Prescott . . . ?" Rosecreek prompted.

He labored to his feet and walked to the tape recorder. "Is there some blank tape on that?"

"Yes," Scott said.

"Look," Rosecreek said, "you have the right—"

"I know. I want to get it over with."

Scott spun the tape and adjusted the recorder. Gardner bent toward it as if addressing a person. He spoke perfunctorily.

"My call to Tina was to ask how she was. She had been terribly depressed. When she called back and asked me to come up to the house, she sounded wild, irresponsible. I was afraid she might do something to herself. When I got there, almost the first thing she demanded was that I marry her. It won't surprise you to hear that she and I had also been—Well, I tried to put her off and quiet her down. But she was beyond reason. Finally I got angry and refused her point-blank. Then she was on me—clawing, pummeling, kicking. I fought back. She grabbed the bookend and raised it with both hands. She was about to slam it down on my head. I grabbed it away and hit her with it, very hard.

"She fell to the floor. There was a lot of blood. I was terrified. I knelt down and tried her pulse. Her heart still seemed to be beating. I went to the phone, thinking to call an ambulance, but I couldn't do it; I was too panicky. I then wiped at the bookend with my handkerchief. I drove back to the marina, praying to God that she was all right, that maybe she'd come to. I called from the booth. There was no answer. I waited and called again. Scott answered and said Tina was dead.

"That's it. I, Gardner Prescott, killed her."

He punched off the recorder and walked back and sat down on the sofa. His blurred eyes rose to meet the sheriff's. He said, his voice uncaring, "You set this all up, didn't you?"

Rosecreek tugged at his cheek. "I'll explain that, Mr. Prescott. The night the papers were planted at the house, a car came shooting past me where I was parked in the trees. I lost it in the fog below, but I'd managed to get the first three numbers on the license plate. The next morning they checked out as Spain's. That satisfied me that he was Mrs. Welles's lover, but it didn't satisfy me he'd killed her. There was too much evidence pointing to Mr. Welles. But then yesterday, Mr. Welles phoned me a transcript of the tape. I asked him to call back in an hour. By then I'd figured out that *two* men must have visited Mrs. Welles that night. From what was on the tape—the business Catherine saw in the study—it seemed a sure thing that the first man was Spain. And it hadn't occurred to me then that maybe *you* and Mrs. Welles . . ." He glanced apologetically at Scott and left the sentence unfinished.

"It took a little more thinking to figure out the second visitor. It seemed unlikely it was Mr. Welles because the car Catherine saw was *leaving* the house. Also, chances are she'd have recognized it if it were her father's. I'm afraid you yourself gave me the answer, Mr. Prescott. Suddenly it dawned on me why you were so frantically determined to clear Mr. Welles and Catherine. There they both were, guilt sticking out all over them—particularly Mr. Welles—and you refused to see it. Then it came to me. Your conscience couldn't accept Mr. Welles or Catherine taking the fall for what you'd done. But it *could* accept someone like Phipps Spain.

"But I couldn't be sure even though we knew you'd talked on the phone to Mrs. Welles. Even though Catherine finally identified that second car as yours. It was still possible that Spain had killed Mrs. Welles and you'd simply discovered the body, or hadn't even gotten into the house. So I decided to get you down here. I knew Spain would follow, we'd been tailing him. With Spain trying to hang it on Welles—who he really believed was the murderer—and you trying to hang it on Spain, I figured there was an outside chance we'd get the truth."

Rosecreek's glance lit for a moment on the yellow kimono. "We got a lot more truth than I bargained for."

Epilogue

the parking area at the foot of Ocean Avenue, turned around and killed the engine. He smoked a cigarette to a stub and ground it out. The blue sedan had not appeared. Still cautious, he drove up Ocean for a

Zurich, 1972

The brown leather arm of the chair had a buttery, almost sensuous, feel under Gardner Prescott's hand. Across the raftered lounge the gleaming crystal behind the softly lit bar seemed to signal a promise of good things to come. Nothing had ever looked so white as the crisp jackets on the attendants. The crackling blaze in the great stone fireplace seemed magical in the way it warmed his right cheek and shoulder.

Only the day before he had walked out the gates of San Quentin, entered the waiting chauffeured car, stopped at a bank, then gone directly to San Francisco airport to catch the flight for Zurich. Arriving, he had checked into the hotel and immediately come here.

Opposite him, his companion observed his look of nostalgia mixed with elation. He said, "I guess you had it pretty rough."

The voice, American as anything heard in a prison yard, sounded amusingly incongruous coming from the plump Japanese face. Gardner had liked him immediately.

"Not too bad," Gardner said. "But thank God it wasn't a worse rap than manslaughter." He waved an arm. "Of course, after three and a half years I began missing this sort of thing. On the other hand, boredom eventually forced me to settle down and finish another book." He sipped his brandy. "But tell me about Scott and Catherine."

"They've got a cottage in Nikko. Very Japanese-y—paper and wood, straw mats, a bonsai garden—the

249

whole bit. Not like my pad in Tokyo. Who wants to be yanking off his shoes all the time? Anyway, Scott's writing stories for kids. Catherine draws the pictures. It's a good setup."

"Sounds like she's adjusted."

"She didn't have to adjust. Those people in Nikko, they don't think she's retarded. They think she's been tapped by the gods to stay a child forever. And the Japanese really dig children."

"Do you see them often?"

"Maybe once a month they take a train down. Stay a few days with us and stop in to see Sinjuko's parents. They're all geat friends."

"What about Sinjuko?"

"I saw her this morning, at the sanatorium here in Zurich. She's still hanging on, but I don't think she'll ever make it out. She knows about Scott and Catherine. And she's very happy for them."

Gardner stared into the fire. "You know, I've often wondered which influenced me more—my caring so much about them or . . . the other incentive."

George Washington Takimoto shrugged. "Why think about it? Now's all that matters. Got any plans?"

"Oh, I'll go on writing, and I expect to travel a lot. This is my first leg on the grand tour."

"Then here's something that should come in handy."

Gardner shifted his gaze back and saw the envelope that was held out to him. It had his name typewritten on it. He took it and expressed his thanks.

He said, "And, of course, I've got something for *you*." He reached inside his dark jacket and drew out a second envelope. "I picked it up from my safe deposit box on the way to the plane. You know the contents, of course."

"More or less. Naturally Scott told me about it."

"Shall we exhume the past?"

"If you mean open it, sure."

Gardner ripped the envelope and slipped out two sheets of paper. Unfolding them and beginning to read, he recalled the frantic emotions that had driven the pen.

To the Sheriff's Office, Marin County, California:

As I write this, my wife, Tina Welles, is lying dead in the study. This will make known the facts surrounding her death.

A short while ago I arrived home from the office and found my wife in an almost hysterical state. She accused me of having an affair with another woman. She was wrong and I told her so. But that didn't calm her, and she then accused me of corrupting our adopted daughter, Catherine. I was thunderstruck, speechless. She lost all control. She leaped at me, scratching and pounding me with her fists. She screamed that she'd divorce me and take everything. I tried to restrain her but couldn't—she'd gone completely berserk. She got hold of the bookend from the desk and raised it over her head to smash me with it. I grabbed for it and we struggled. She kept cursing me and shouting that she'd take Catherine away and I'd never again see her. I must have gone mad. By then I had the bookend and I slammed her with it.

The next thing I knew I was in the downstairs bathroom rinsing blood from my hands. When I went back into the study my wife was dead. Then I went to my daughter's room. She was in shock, and I can only surmise that she witnessed some or all of the violence. Then Gardner Prescott phoned. I told him Tina had been murdered and asked him to come to the house. When he arrived he said that he had called earlier in the evening and that Tina told him she'd phone back. When she did she was hysterical and said she wanted to see him right away. But when he reached the house he could hear us shouting and didn't want to come in. So he drove back to the marina but began to fear something terrible had happened. That's why he had called me.

Gardner Prescott told me all this as soon as he entered the house. I was terrified. Not just for myself, God knows, but for Catherine. If I should go to jail, she'd have no one to care for her. I told this to Gardner and he was deeply sympathetic. So sympathetic that I began to see a possible way out. I made him these propositions:

1. I would pay him $50,000 if he would remain silent while we hoped the police would blame Tina's death on a prowler.
2. I would pay him $100,000 if he would accept the guilt should it appear certain I would be exposed.

Gardner Prescott has agreed to this. I am giving this letter to him as a bond, so that he'll have no fear I'll welsh on the deal. Should I fail to pay, he can turn this letter over to the police.

I know that will never become necessary. But should the authorities somehow discover this confession, I can only hope to God that the circumstances I've described will cause them to see the killing of my wife for what it was—not a premeditated murder, but a tragic accident.

Scott Welles

Gardner handed the letter to Tak, who read it slowly. He looked up, shaking his head. "Christ, and Catherine still thinks it was you."

"That's really the only bad part—I can never see them." Gardner reflected. "There was a chance she might have wondered about Scott, I think, if she'd heard his car come in that night. But at that moment, her head was buried under the blankets. And as it turned out, all she heard from the study was Tina ranting and raving."

He mused for a moment. "What a hell of a decision that must have been for Scott to make—taking Catherine to that doctor, I mean. Think of the risk. But he had to find out what she'd seen and heard.

"Anyway, when Scott told me the business about Tina accusing him of having another woman, I assumed he was referring to Sinjuko—Tina had more than briefed me about her. The situation with Catherine, of course, never came out until much, much later. After it was all over, Scott told me exactly what Tina had threatened to do to Catherine. 'I'll take that little whore and lock her away' and 'She'll rot in an institution with all the other idiots.' Stuff like that. No wonder he flipped."

Tak squinted an almond eye. "That bit about Scott corrupting Catherine. Does it mean Tina knew they'd already been . . . together?"

"Damned if I know, but I'm guessing yes. Tina had always been neurotically jealous of the affection Scott and Catherine shared. She knew Catherine had seen pictures of Sinjuko and had read a story about her and Scott—a love story—that he'd written after he came back from Japan. Tina had even overheard Scott in the study calling someone his lovely geisha. At the time, she thought he was on the phone wih Sinjuko. So once Scott had exploded the Sinjuko myth, all these things must have rushed back to Tina. Throw in a little feminine intuition and it's easy to see how she guessed that Catherine and Scott had been, as you say, together. She was a desperately unhappy woman to begin with, and this must have blown her mind."

"Quite a story," Tak said, sipping his brandy. "And what happened to her boyfriend?"

"Nothing. The sheriff never pressed charges of any kind. Must have figured the poor bastard had already taken enough of a beating."

Gardner shifted uncomfortably in his chair. "You know, when Scott and I made our deal, neither of us had any idea Tina'd had a lover. As soon as that popped up, I have to admit I broke my back trying to make a case against the guy—crime of passion, that sort of thing. So as much as I fancy the self-sacrificing hero role, the truth is I'd have been damned glad to let him take the rap instead of me."

"Hell, I don't know that I blame you."

"I've had a long time to think about it, Tak. Maybe it sounds phony to say so now, but I'm glad things worked out as they did."

Tak finished the rest of his brandy. "Anyway, it doesn't matter now, so what's the difference?"

Gardner opened the envelope Tak had given him and scanned the certified check made out for one hundred thousand dollars signed by Scott Welles. He slipped it into his pocket.

Tak fanned the air with the letter. "Scott says he never wants to see this."

"Okay, why not a burial?"

Tak signaled a waiter and ordered champagne. They waited until it had been popped and poured and they were alone.

"Cremation?" Tak asked.

"Exactly what I had in mind."

Tak tossed the letter on the fire. They watched it flame and blacken and curl and turn to ashes.

"Justice," Gardner said wryly. "You can't always trust it to the law books."

Tak raised his bubbling glass. "To freedom."

Gardner clicked his glass against Tak's and smiled. "*Kampai!*" he said.

"A spine-tingling page turner."
—Mary Higgins Clark,
author of <u>Where Are The Children?</u>

CECILIA BARTHOLOMEW

A four-year-old boy is found dead. His eight-year-old sister, Billyjean, is accused of the murder. This is the story of Billyjean—thirteen years later.

Now she is twenty-one, and going home. She had finally confessed to killing her brother. That showed she could face reality. She could live on the outside.

But Billyjean didn't really remember killing her brother, no matter what she confessed—and someone else knew that too!

She had outrun the dark.... and now she must run for her life!

$2.25   B12046488
Available wherever paperbacks are sold.

NT-34